THE LONG WALK BACK

RACHEL DOVE

B
Boldwood

First published in 2018. This edition published in 2024 in Great Britain by Boldwood Books Ltd.

Cover Design by Colin Thomas

Cover Photography: Colin Thomas

This book is a work of fiction and, except in the case of historical fact, any resemblance to actual persons, living or dead, is purely coincidental.

Every effort has been made to obtain the necessary permissions with reference to copyright material, both illustrative and quoted. We apologise for any omissions in this respect and will be pleased to make the appropriate acknowledgements in any future edition.

A CIP catalogue record for this book is available from the British Library.

Paperback ISBN 978-1-83617-765-4

Large Print ISBN 978-1-83617-766-1

Hardback ISBN 978-1-83617-764-7

Ebook ISBN 978-1-83617-767-8

Kindle ISBN 978-1-83617-768-5

Audio CD ISBN 978-1-83617-759-3

MP3 CD ISBN 978-1-83617-760-9

Digital audio download ISBN 978-1-83617-761-6

Boldwood Books Ltd
23 Bowerdean Street
London SW6 3TN
www.boldwoodbooks.com

To my husband Peter, who never reads my books, but inspires them anyway.
Thank you for putting up with me.

PROLOGUE

That day will stay with me forever. It shaped me for every day that followed, that's for certain. That day I learned an answer to one of mankind's big questions: what do you see when your body is at the point of death? What do you feel when your body begins to stop fighting?

Not your average day. Or not the average day that civilians experienced, anyway. War tended to put a slightly different spin on things. Once the rose-tinted glasses came off, they just didn't seem to fit the same way after.

An average day is going to work, coming home, parking on the couch in front of the TV, a takeaway perched on your knee while you moan to yourself about how skint you are, how the country is going to the dogs, how much you might hate your job. Your commute. Your neighbour who lets his dog pee on your front steps or bark into the early hours. That's an average day, one that blends into countless others through the years, till you wake up in your fifties, bored, bald and fat, wondering at what point the dreams of your younger self went down the toilet. At least, that's the way I saw things. That was never going to be me, I'd decided early in life. So I made different choices. Those choices led me to that day, what looked like my last day. Karma is a bitch; I hear you on that one. I can still remember every detail.

An hour earlier, I'd been carrying out a routine sweep of the area with my unit. Of my thirty-one years on the earth, I'd spent fifteen of them in the army. We were out in Iraq, pushing back the small group of terror cells that threatened the small villages we were camped near to. Many of the villagers wanted us here, but tensions were rising. You could feel it ratcheting up, like the daily heat when the sun broke over the horizon.

It's not like on the news. You think it all looks the same. Desert, broken buildings, busted vehicles, shattered people. Aid trucks surrounded by soldiers and desperate people. That's all there, but it's far from everything else I'd seen on my tour. There is no beauty on the news, but it exists here. We fear what we don't know, what we can't control; but here, people live the same as us in many ways. The ways that mattered. I have seen family photos hung on walls, gardens lovingly tended, children loved and cared for. The actions of a few causes the outcome for many, and I saw it every day. I joined to serve, to have a purpose, but I also enlisted to find the family I never had. So now I fought for them too, with them by my side.

There had been a lot of unease the last few weeks, and you could feel the stress, the taut emotions of both the people and the enemy, even through the hot, dry air. I had had a bad feeling in the pit of my gut for days. When the shots had begun firing, I knew why. They had been gearing up to take us down, and as prepared as we thought we were, as prepared as *I* thought we were, we were still caught with our pants down that day.

'Pull back!' I boomed gruffly to my charges. 'Come on, go, go, go!' I started to run for the nearest building, the one we had just finished sweeping. It was abandoned, full of empty makeshift housing, food rotting on tables that would never host a family meal again. I kept looking over my shoulder, watching my guys take shelter one by one. A hail of shots whizzed past my ear, and I threw myself against the side of the nearest abandoned car. Hunching down, I scanned the landscape to where the shots were coming from. Two of my guys were still on the way to the shelter – one hunched over, not moving. The other, Travis, was dragging him to safety. Blood followed them like a trail of gunpowder as they desperately tried to get to cover. Another barrage of shots rang out, giving away their location, and Travis jerked. He'd been hit, but he kept going, pulling Smithy along with him, hung over his shoulder. *They weren't going to make it.* I jumped up, firing a volley off at the top of the building, but the enemy fired back. *Shit.* Hunching down again, I shouted at Travis to get a move on, grabbing my radio and running towards them.

'Hightower, can you see him yet?' I shouted into the radio. Bradley, my sniper on the opposite set of flat roofs, was my ace in the hole. If he had a clear shot, he would already have executed it. 'Got a shot?'

'Nearly, the slippery bastard is hidden well. He has a kid up there with him, using him as a shield.'

I cursed under my breath. I reached Travis and grabbed Smithy from him. Travis was bleeding badly, but it looked like a shoulder wound. Through and through, judging from the blood he'd left in his wake.

We ran hell for leather towards the shelter, Hightower screaming into the radio.

'He's reloading Coop, get a move on!'

I was almost at the shelter, Travis was just ahead,
racing to get ready to help Smithy, who was still out
cold. My muscles burned from the effort of dragging
him along with me, but I ignored the pain, pushing on.

'Almost there,' I shouted back into the receiver. 'Is
the kid armed?'

'Negative,' Hightower boomed back. 'Human
shield.'

'Then we wait till it's clear. No collateral. You
copy?' A difficult call when my men were taking hits,
but that was the job. I had to make them, and hope to
God the delay wouldn't cost my men their lives.

'Copy,' Hightower confirmed.

'Find a shot, and take him down!'

Hightower acknowledged and just as we reached
the lip of the shelter, shots rang out again, this time
with the 'phut phut' of the sniper rifle as Hightower
followed orders. I was just wondering whether the
poor child on the roof was okay, when a huge force
pushed me straight off my feet, into the air. Teeth rat-
tling in my skull, I reached out to tighten my grip on
Smithy, but felt nothing but space. Hitting the ground,

I struggled for breath, dust and debris raining down around me. Hightower was screaming down the air waves, mobilising the others in my unit.

I struggled to breathe, my mouth coated with a new layer of dust every time I managed to pull in a ragged breath. I could hear the commotion around me and moved my head to the side to look for Smithy. I could see him a few feet away, and I knew without a doubt he was dead. I turned away, already wanting to erase the memory of his crumpled form from my memory. I coughed, and felt a warm trickle run down my cheek. Not good, I thought to myself, even as the blood took some of the dust with it. I could hear my friends, my comrades in arms, running towards me, firing shots off, barking orders at each other. Pain. Pain was the thing I felt the most, but I couldn't pinpoint where. It was everywhere. In every cell of my prone body. But that was it. Pain, noise, panic in the voices around me as they grew closer.

There was no white light, no images of me running around in short trousers playing in my head, nothing. I couldn't see anything but dust, flashes of weaponry, and the smell of action and desperation in the air. I felt bone tired, a blanket of fatigue covering me from head to foot. A little voice inside, telling me to sleep. *Time to rest now, soldier.* I tried to shake my head, keep myself awake, but the warm feeling continued to spread through me. Numbing every place it touched. My body wasn't responding. It was like slipping into a hot bath after a long, cold day. I could feel my muscles began to relax, and my throat filling up with liquid. I tried to spit, to turn my head, but my eyelids were already fluttering. I thought of the kid on the rooftop. I wondered if he had parents around, people who were searching for their child, missing him. I wondered who would miss me and came up empty. My hesitation had caused this. Not taking the quicker shot might have cost my team dearly and be the end of me. But if that child lived to see another sunrise over me, I could live with that. The cost of war had to be paid sometime. *I hope my team gets out.* And that's the last thing I remember, laying there with blood gurgling in my throat. Hoping that my brothers in arms made it home. That the boy on the rooftop would have a better ending to his story. That was worth dying for.

1

Kate was pulling funny faces into the camera when the call came in to tell her casualties were en route. She turned around to face the opposite direction, shielding her son from the images of people running behind her.

'Sorry, bud. Mummy has to go now, but I will call you back as soon as I can, yeah? Remind Dad to take you to football practice after school, okay?' Her son rolled his eyes.

'He never checks the calendar Mum, you know that. When are you coming home?' Her colleague, Trevor tapped her on the arm, waving to her son's image on the phone screen.

'Hey Jamie, good luck at practice! Kate, we have to

go,' he said, frowning in apology. From the look on his face, it was bad. She held her easy smile in place, blew a kiss at her son. Jamie rolled his eyes but blew one back.

'I'm eight, Mum. When I'm nine there are no more kisses, okay? It's well embarrassing!'

Kate laughed. 'No deal, kiddo. I will still be wanting kisses when you are all grown up. I have to go, see you soon. Love you.'

Jamie smiled weakly. She knew that this was hard for him too, being separated for so long, but she couldn't miss the opportunity to do her job in the field. 'Love you too, Mum,' he said, and his face disappeared from view as the call ended. She knew he would understand better when he was older. When he knew more about the world, other than his relatively sheltered life back home. She hoped that he would be proud that his mother went out there to the places on the news, did what she could to help. Did something with her life; that he would remember that instead of the times she worked late, went away, was an absent parent. Mothers were a different breed to fathers. Fathers could have it all, but mothers were judged no matter what they did. Working, not working. She loved Jamie, but when she stood there in a messy house, with leaking breasts and a screaming newborn, she knew it would never be enough. Perhaps if her marriage had been a happier one, she might have felt more settled. Not that she blamed anyone for that. Sometimes circumstances didn't add up. Not everything could be roses over the door. She wasn't naïve enough to think it was as simple as all that. Life was messy and relying on another person for happiness never ended well. It had to come from within. She loved Jamie dearly. He was her world, but she still wanted the moon and the stars. Men could have all that and no one batted an eyelid. A woman wanting to do the same? Judgement would follow. She wanted to be there for him, and for herself. She wanted Jamie to grow up in a world where that particular glass ceiling was gone, replaced by open sky. If she could help smash it, all the better. She would make it up to him when she got back, she told herself. Forgetting entirely that she'd come here to escape other things, too. Like his father, and the dying embers of their marriage.

Kate threw the phone into her bag, grabbed her scrubs after throwing her clothes onto her cot bed and got herself ready in record time. Grabbing her kit, she raced to follow Trevor to the hospital tent nearby. She covered her eyes as best she could from the dust that the incoming helicopter kicked up in the sandy dirt that their medical camp was perched on.

Doing a three-month stint with the Red Cross as a trauma surgeon was not for the faint-hearted, but Kate Harper loved every bloody minute of it. She had two weeks left, and although she missed her boy dearly, she knew that going home to her usual hospital job would be an adjustment. Not as much as it would be going home to Neil, her husband of seven years. She had to admit to herself, the distance between them lately mounted up to more than miles, and she didn't quite know what to do about it. Well, that wasn't true. She knew what to do, but the thought of having to face her son and tell him his parents were better off apart made her shudder. She was used to overcoming trauma, not inflicting it. Especially not to her favourite person in the world. The thought of seeing Neil again, having that talk, filled her with anxiety. She knew that this trip hadn't been the only cause that changed something between them, but it had stretched the elastic of their relationship so thin it was essentially broken. She wasn't sure it could ever be fixed. Being here, with time away and perspective to think had served to confirm that she didn't want to. She didn't miss him. There was no longing for him. She couldn't remember a time she had. Their relationship wasn't one borne out of passion. Practicality more like. Not exactly the stuff of love stories. Coming to a battlefield, she'd realised that not only had she left one at home, but she felt more herself away from her other half. The silent recriminations between them that hung like axes in the air, just waiting to drop and finally cleave them apart. Something that the distance and circumstance was doing a good job of already.

Being here was a very different kind of working away. Their phone calls were always snatched seconds. When she did get time to call, the signal often dropped, leaving them to play frustrated phone tag with each other. When he was away for work at conferences, they could chat leisurely, not that they had for a long time. Him from his safe snug hotel room at the side of some motorway. Her from their bed, with their son sleeping soundly nearby. Not that it would have helped. Their conversations back then still only consisted of errands to run, Jamie's school day, their workdays. The logistics of their married life together. Here, the calls were clipped, short. Checking in. Are you and Jamie okay? Is it bad there? She couldn't talk about her day. What would she tell him? All about the lives she saved? The ones she lost? She didn't want to think about them, let alone try to form words, to explain them to a man who worked in a safe office all day, watching the clock for meeting times, not for giving time of death.

It narrowed their conversation topics to near nothing. She couldn't help but feel mad if he moaned about his day, about things that Kate had already realised didn't matter in the grand scheme. Neil got mad that she was so closed off and cagey about her life there. Other times she could feel the resentment in his voice, as though she were away on a girly holiday and he had been left holding the pre-teen. They could fill a book with everything they couldn't say. She couldn't remember the last time she had told him she loved him – or felt it. The wind picked up, jolting her back to where she could help. She pushed her marriage to the back of her mind, she had to work now. Some puzzles were easier to solve than others.

The chopper landed, the metal glinting in the early morning scorch of the sun. Kate grabbed her hair, pulling it tighter into her ponytail, and raced to meet the stretcher. She snapped a pair of gloves on as she ran, though she wasn't sure how sterile they would be given the sand flying around. Her colleagues at home would balk at some of the makeshift operations set up in these tents. The medicine was the key though, patching people up, getting them home. The rest was done as best they could under the circumstances. It wasn't all pretty and clean here. In this environment, fighting death was bloody, messy and fast. Split second decisions were crucial.

'What do we have?'

'My Captain,' a hulking man jumped out, addressing her in clipped, terse tones. 'It's bad, Doc, you gotta save him.' A wiry scrap of a boy was wrapped in a blanket in his bulky arms, his little fingers gripping the emblem on the man's uniform as he looked at her, wide eyed. *Sniper.*

'Whose child is this?' She asked, seeing there were no other civilians with them. Just a gurney bearing a man who looked like he'd been ripped apart. Her eyes flicked away from the body bag she saw in the back. *Focus on the living.*

'We don't know, insurgents were using him as a shield. He's not injured.' The man shot back, moving out of the way as his captain was brought out. 'Captain made the call to save him, bastards had us before we knew it.' The boy whimpered in his arms, and he lowered his voice to a dull roar. 'He can't die, you hear me?'

Kate didn't reply, turning to the army medic pulling the patient out on the gurney, keeping his head dipped below the spinning chopper blades. 'Run it down for me.' Shorthand for their kind of patient handover.

'One dead in the field, two injured; one in the other chopper incoming. This one is Captain Thomas Cooper, his unit was ambushed. Multiple injuries, IED, left leg. Flatlined twice on the way here, his vitals are shot. He has shrapnel injuries to his leg and torso; he hasn't been conscious since we got him out of there.' The medic glanced across at her. 'We need to move fast.' Kate nodded, running alongside the trolley as they raced for the trauma tent.

'What meds has he had?'

'We started him on a course of strong antibiotics and 10 mg of morphine. We had no time for anything else, we had to get him out of there.'

It didn't look good. Captain Cooper's eyes fluttered, and Kate noticed what a beautiful shade of green they were, the contrast made all the starker against his deathly pale skin and blood-splattered face.

His lips moved, but she couldn't make out the rasping sounds he tried to form.

'Captain.' She leaned closer. 'Try not to speak. We got you.'

His pupils were wide, darkness against the emerald green surrounding them. He grabbed at the bottom hem of her top with a shaky hand, and when she reached for it, his fingers locked around hers. Gripping her tight. His hand was huge, dwarfing hers in its grasp. She waited for the pain of his panicked hold, but it was gentle, insistent.

'No.' He tried to shake his head. 'Leave me.' He coughed, blood dripping from the corner of his mouth. 'Kid... rooftop. Save... him.' His eyes grew less focused, glassy. 'Smithy...' He lost the fight for consciousness.

'Move!' Kate boomed. 'Faster!' His grip didn't leave her, and she held his hand, gripping the gurney and running flat out. They raced into the tent, transferring him from the stretcher to one of the hospital treatment tables. He never made a murmur. Resting his hand by his side, Kate grabbed a pair of scissors from her kit and cut away the remnants of his trousers, showing torn black boxers underneath. His left leg was a bloody mess. They had to stop the bleeding, or he would lose his life too. Looking at his right leg, she saw shrapnel protruding from his bloody wounds. These were comparatively superficial wounds; had he not been running flat out, she surmised that both legs would have hit the homemade bomb and been in the same state. The only reason this soldier had any leg at all was the position of his running body as the blast hit. She got to work, barking out orders to the staff running around the bed next to her. The whole tent was a hive of activity, and Kate blocked the noises out.

The sniper was trying to push his way through, another soldier holding him back. Shouting at him to keep it together. Let them work. She switched it all off, focused on what was in front of her.

On her first week here, she had been useless. She was no stranger to traumatic injuries, but the relative silence of the wards and operating rooms back home was a world apart from the sounds that surrounded her on a daily basis now. Strapping grown men, screaming, calling for their mothers, their wives, their gods. Helicopters and the booming sounds of bombs nearby, gunfire in the distance. All of these sounds had taken some adjustment, but now she tuned them out, was able to concentrate on what her colleagues were saying, the heart sounds she listened to in damaged chests, the gurgles and moans from the bodies she tended to. Kate ran over to Trevor, who'd just run in with the other chopper casualty.

'The captain's not looking good. We need to stop the bleeders in his chest and right leg too. He's lost a lot of blood. You got this?'

Trevor nodded, working fast as he listened to his colleague and one-time student.

'I'm good.' As she turned to run back, he shouted after her.

'Kate, save him if you can. He saved two others in

the field, his troop only made it out because of his actions. He made a difficult call, saving the kid too. Only one of his men died, and he will be angry enough about that when he comes to. It could have been a bloodbath. The guy was bleeding out and he still gave the order to get the boy from the rooftop the second his team got to him, they defied his order to leave him in the field. If it was up to him, he wouldn't have been here, with a chance. We owe it to him to get him through this.'

Kate ignored the slab of thick tension that nestled in her throat. 'Roger that.'

'They used a kid as a human shield, Kate. An innocent fucking child. No one else gets to die today.' Kate looked at Cooper as she worked to stem the bleeding. She thought of her earlier phone call with her son. Worrying about him missing football practice, whether he had eaten breakfast. A world away from being used as a weapon in a war he didn't cause or belong in. A mother had almost lost her child today. Thanks to this man, he was here. Safe. The army could get him out of there, out of this. Wouldn't she want the same if her child was out there? It made her speed up. Every second mattered, and she vowed to give the battle-ravaged man more time on this earth, no matter what.

'Sniper,' she called to the man still trying to force his way through to the captain.

'They call me Hightower, ma'am.' Addressing him had stilled him momentarily in his efforts to get across the room.

'Yeah, well no one calls me that, Hightower. Doctor, usually, or Kate.' He clenched his jaw, giving her a slow acknowledging nod. 'I got this, okay?' She looked him dead in the eye. 'I am going to save your captain, so stand down. Take the child to be checked over in the triage tent.' When he didn't move, she levelled him with a stare. 'Now, Hightower. Go.'

When he left the tent, Trevor shot her a grateful look.

'Glad you're here, badass. You heard her, team! No one else is dying today. Get to it.'

* * *

Hours later, the tent was quieter, calmer. The gunfire in the far distance had abated; the silence almost eerie in comparison. Kate was exhausted, covered in dirt and grime that had mixed with the sweat of her frantic exertion to save lives in the middle of a warzone. They needed to be rested, ever ready at a moment's notice, but the adrenaline of the last few hours had kicked in now. She knew if she went to bed, she would just lay awake staring at the ceiling of the tent, so she stayed. Sarah Fielding, a combat medic assigned to this unit, was at a nearby desk sorting through personal effects ready to bag and tag. They tried to save what they could, to either give back to the soldiers, or send back to their families should the worst happen. Kate went to the small kitchen area and grabbed a strong coffee, sitting down on a chair near the desk.

'Hi Sarah, you okay?' Kate asked tentatively, sipping at the strong hot drink. She felt the jolt of caffeine lick through her limbs.

'Yeah, I just hate this job,' Sarah replied, frowning. Kate noticed a familiar piece of clothing.

'That the captain's trousers? Mind if I look?'

Sarah shrugged, attempting to stifle a yawn and failing. 'No, bag it up for me would you, when you're done? I still have a pile to get through but I need to get my head down.' Sarah looked across at her, smiling weakly. 'You should too, you look done in.'

Kate shrugged, taking the possessions from her colleague. 'I will, I can't settle yet. You go.'

Sarah placed a hand on her shoulder as she passed, squeezing it in appreciation. 'Night, Kate.'

'Night, Sarah,' Kate said over her shoulder. The captain was still unconscious, whether from the sedation or his injuries remained to be seen. They had stopped the bleeding and he was stable. For now. Glugging at her coffee, she set it down on the desk and started to go through her patient's belongings. He had the usual field stuff in his pockets, along with a wallet. It had escaped the blast intact. His mobile phone was shattered, so she itemised it and put it into the bag. Opening the wallet, she looked through the contents, feeling guilty for going through his personal possessions, but it needed to be done. Sometimes, all families got back were the contents of their loved one's pockets and bags, and even a half-eaten packet of mints was a comfort to a grieving mother. Photos and letters were the gold though. Looking through the wallet, she found amongst the cards and money a little stack of snaps. She frowned as she thumbed through them. They were all of him and his friends, in various barracks and war zones. No family pictures, no smiling mother and father, no rosy-cheeked children cuddled by a proud wife. She observed how handsome he was, those penetrating green eyes she couldn't help but notice. Smiling into the camera, laughing into another. His playful side showed, a man goofing around with his buddies in a rare peaceful moment. She wondered whether anyone would be trying to ring his phone. Worrying about why he didn't answer.

Trevor came into the room, unnoticed by Kate till he took a sip of her now lukewarm coffee.

'Hey,' she said teasingly. 'Get your own!'

Trevor winked and drained the cup. 'You should be in bed. Want a fresh one?'

Kate nodded, already back to being absorbed in the images in her hands. 'Do you know the captain?'

'Thomas Cooper, one of the good ones,' Trevor replied. 'How's he doing?'

Kate looked at Trevor, a frown on her tired face. 'Stable. For now. His leg doesn't look good. We're watching him for signs of sepsis. The child he saved is doing well. Shaken but unharmed.'

'Difficult call to make,' Trevor murmured, his voice quiet. 'Hightower was in agreement that he did the right thing. The soldier who died was in bad shape, I don't think he'd have made it either way. Sounds like he was a sitting duck. Cooper would have lost more men if he hadn't strode in himself.' He finished off the mug. 'Fucking IEDs. They got him here quick, but...' His lips pursed. 'He won't be happy if he can't go back into full service. Has he woken up yet?'

Kate shook her head. Trevor's gaze dropped.

'Has he got any family?' Kate asked. 'There are only his army buddies in these photos.'

Trevor shook his head. 'Nope, Cooper is army born and bred. No family to speak of, as far as I know. He keeps his cards pretty close to his chest.'

Kate put the photos back, finishing her task and tying the bag up to go with the others. He was alone then, like her. His team were his family, his brothers. He'd strode right into danger to pull them out. Made the call to save a child even when the safer, quicker action would be to neutralise the threat no matter what. That little boy would get to live, to recover, thanks to the man in the bed nearby. A man from the other side of the world had given him a future, a chance. A man like that should have someone in his corner back home, eager to see him come back. Thinking of those green eyes in the photos, she wondered why this man had gotten under her skin. She'd seen dozens of soldiers here, and never pondered their back stories. It bothered her, for some reason, that he might not have anything to return to. Maybe it was because the boy he'd saved had made her think of her own son, safe and sound back home. Shielded from the horrors of here. Maybe it was thinking of what she had to face when her plane landed. Being alone herself, even as she yearned for her marriage to finally be over in *every sense*. Except she did have people, Jamie. Waiting for her, counting on her to return to them. From peeking into Cooper's life, she knew in her bones that his comrades were all he had. If he returned home, and couldn't be a soldier any more, what would be left for him back home? Who would be there to make those green eyes lose the haunting look she'd spied when he'd looked at her, eyelids flickering as they tried to focus? To soothe that deep frown he had, even in sleep? She looked at the ward entrance, partitioned off by canvas doors.

Trevor went off to get more coffee, but when he came back, Kate was nowhere to be seen. He carried the cups through to the main ward tent, sure that a nurse would be grateful for the hot drink. Walking through, something made him slow his heavy step. At the end of the ward, next to Captain Cooper's bed, Kate lay in a chair, one hand over his. 'Kate?'

She didn't move, her eyes still fixed on the sleeping Captain. 'Kate? You should try to sleep.'

She turned to look at her boss, her hand still holding Cooper's. 'Do you think he has anyone, back home I mean? His wallet didn't show any personal life?'

Trevor frowned. 'Not sure, I only know him by reputation. Why? You don't usually ask.'

She gave a slow shrug. 'I know. I think it's the kid. You know, he didn't ask about himself once. He was only concerned for everyone else.'

Trevor didn't say anything at first. 'Don't stay up too long,' were his parting words as he pushed the coffee cup into her free hand. She drank it slowly, watching his vitals and wishing they looked better. He was in bad shape. The cup was almost empty when she felt his fingers tighten around hers.

'The... kid,' he croaked out as she dumped the cup to one side. Checked the monitors for any disturbing flickers.

'Safe, unharmed,' she told him. 'Your team got out too.' The crease in his brows abated a little, and she squeezed his fingers. 'You did good, Captain.' His green eyes opened a little wider. 'Do you have anyone at home? I mean, anyone I could call?' The resounding shake of his head was unmistakable. 'Rest now,' she told him, looking at the monitor, not sure what else she could tell him. *I'm alone, like you? Married to the job? No. Their circumstances weren't the same.* 'I have a little boy,' she said instead. 'If he were on a rooftop, I would hope for someone like you to be there, too.' She turned back, but he was asleep once more.

2

FOUR MONTHS EARLIER

'And what about Jamie, Kate? Have you thought about him in all this? I have a job too, you know,' Neil said, ripping off his tie and slamming it down on the table that sat in their large open-plan kitchen. Kate continued to stir the pasta, giving herself a minute before acknowledging her husband's rant. These days, it was the only way they communicated at all.

She turned down the stove and moved to face him, resting her back against the kitchen worktop. The room was dimly lit, the side bulbs under the units giving off a glow to light up the space. One of Jamie's school projects lay on the table, drying papier-mâché planets, laid on old newspaper, ready to paint.

Looking at her husband, Kate noticed the fine lines around his eyes, the crinkles on his forehead. When they had first got together, she had never imagined that it would end up like this. No matter their struggles, they always got on. Could talk to each other. Tell the other how they were feeling. It was, she'd thought as good a foundation as any way for a life together.

She'd fancied him rotten from the second she set eyes on him, and they had both enjoyed the other's company. The attraction was there, he was open, funny, caring. It had started off so well she didn't think it would be anything but good. But then the initial spark had cooled. Lust did that sometimes, like an attendee at a masquerade ball pretending to be something deeper. Till the mask of that initial have-to-have-you-now receded like an ocean tide.

In reality, outside the bedroom, they were very different people, and Kate was getting ready to break it off, realising that their relationship wasn't lighting the spark she had expected to feel. They'd perhaps rushed into something more than it was meant to be. Had they just kept dating, and not named what they were to each other, it would have been easier. She was busy with work, so was he. She figured it would have been better not to force something that wasn't a forever kind of deal. They were opposites, people who'd collided, enjoyed each other. She could pull back and let things run their natural course.

Then she was late. Four weeks overdue on her normally regular cycle, and she just knew. A few weeks before, determined to give her boyfriend a good opportunity to bowl her over again, to see for herself what was and could be between them, she had suggested a night on the town. It had gone quite well too, their little pauses in conversation less obvious, but Kate had drunk a lot that night, determined to silence the voice inside her that told her that this guy was not the one for her. Everyone deserved a chance. The next morning, she had woken up with a thick head, a heavy heart and a naked Neil sleeping beside her. And it was too late. Her attempts at silencing the voice had failed. Right along with the contraception. She was the original cliché, knocked-up after their night together.

That definitely hadn't been part of her plans, especially as she had just secured her dream job as an orthopaedic surgeon at the local hospital in Leeds. Whether she liked it or not, she'd have to juggle a baby and her career, and a partner who had just been cemented into her life. She'd had options, of course. She could have raised the baby alone. Told him of her doubts, but he was a good man, she liked him, they had chemistry. She told herself that she could at least try. Life wasn't all perfect matches and fairy tales. Fair from it. Abortion wasn't an option for Kate; she had no problem with people having a choice, supported it, but her choice was to keep the baby, no matter how inconvenient the timing was.

So, they'd gotten married. Neil had been delighted, never sharing her worries or misgivings. Being from a large family, he saw this as the way life was supposed to be; meet someone, get married, have a baby. By the time Jamie came along, they had bought a house together and settled down into the rut that was to be their married life. And a rut it was for Kate. In many ways, she loved being with him. He was a good father, he loved her, they got on, but the thunderbolt was never there for her. She knew it was for him, he told her how he felt all the time. Perhaps her indifference over the years was what killed any remnant they had of the early days and weeks. All she knew was, she had tried.

Surgeons have a reputation for being rather cold, clinical people. Top-of-their-field surgeons are pretty much left alone. They cut and save lives, they don't get emotionally invested in their patients. Neil saw how Kate was with her work, and took it as an extension of her. It wasn't a reflection on their marriage, their child, their life together. It was just the prism of her work that distorted how she viewed everything else. At first, Kate convinced herself of the same. It was the stress of juggling this new life, raising the person they made together whilst still putting in the hours. It was a lot for anyone to shoulder. Balls got dropped, kicked under the couch and left to gather dust.

As time went on, they settled into each other's lives, forging one of their own. Kate knew that her love for Jamie was one of the things Neil adored most about her. There, she came alive for him and shed the surgeon skin. And in the beginning, that was enough for him. It worked, till it didn't, and he grew resentful of the person she'd always been.

Kate adored her child from day one. Even looking at Jamie now, she was hit by a sucker punch of emotion, a protective instinct that she'd never known she had. Jamie was her world, and now Neil was using that to sling mud at her from across the room. Looking at Neil across the kitchen, she wondered how many of those lines and wrinkles had been caused by her over the years. He seemed to age before her eyes, and she considered what another woman might have seen when looking at him. Maybe she would have loved him more. He could have been someone's first choice. Did he know now that he wasn't hers?

'Are you going to answer me? I'm not one of your lackies, Kate!'

Kate's head whipped round, her levels of fury rising. He had a chip on his shoulder about her job, and it was raising its ugly green head more and more these days.

'Don't talk to me like that, Neil! Of course I don't want to leave Jamie, but Trevor asked me to help. It's a short-term placement, the learning opportunities would be amazing, and I can really help people over there!'

Neil snorted. 'Oh yes, you get to swoop in with your superhero cape, save some soldiers, whilst I stay home, play nanny and then hear nothing but how great you are from everyone we know. Your mother thinks I'm a joke!'

Kate shook her head, shooting daggers at him from across the room. 'My mother says no such thing, that's all in your own head for God's sake, and you'll hardly be a nanny. Jamie's at school full-time, and he's no bother. Besides, you are his father! And please keep your voice down, that son you care so much about is upstairs asleep.'

Neil grabbed his keys from the sideboard and stormed across the kitchen.

'Where are you going now? I made dinner!' Kate said to his retreating form.

'Well, plate it up, Supergirl!' he said sarcastically, and the front door slammed shut. Kate turned off the heat, and picking up the pan, tipped the contents straight into the kitchen bin. She filled the pan with water and left it in the sink. Heading to the fridge, she picked out the bottle of chardonnay she had left in there and poured herself a stiff glass. It tasted tart on her tongue, and followed up with a gentle lick at her tensed up muscles.

'Mum?' Whirling around, Kate saw her son, Jamie, stood there, hair all messy tufts, clad in his favourite onesie. Putting the glass down, she walked over to her child.

'You should be in bed, sweetheart,' she chided.

'Was that dad slamming the door? What's wrong?' he asked, his brow furrowed.

'He didn't mean to, darling. Nothing's wrong, he just forgot something at work.'

Jamie nodded, his wide eyes looking at her in question. Kate gave him a squeeze.

'Come on, don't worry. Everything's fine, let's get you a glass of milk and back to bed.'

Once Jamie was sleeping again, Kate tidied away the rest of the dinner things and poured herself another glass of wine. It was after eleven, and Neil still hadn't come home or phoned. His sulks could take a while, and he had even taken to sleeping at the office some nights, or on a mate's couch. Picking up her mobile phone, she dialled his number. It rang and rang; she was about to hang up when he answered.

'What?' he said flatly. 'If it's not about Jamie, I'm not in the mood to talk.'

'What happened to us, Neil?' she asked, her voice small, sounding needy in her own ears. 'We used to get on so well. We can't go on like this.'

A sigh came down the line. 'Get on? That's the problem, Kate. You always make us sound like friends. You don't need me, do you? Not really. I used to think what we had was enough, but I don't think we can get by on good enough any more. You don't need me at all.'

'Of course I do,' she replied, frowning at his question. 'We both need you.'

'No, that's not what I mean. We have a life together, but you've never really needed me, have you? Wanted me even? Tell me, if something bad happened, who would you ring first?'

'You,' she said. 'You're my husband, of course it

would be you. Neil, I've never lied to you about who I am, or how I feel. I... care for you.' She closed her eyes. She couldn't say she loved him any more. Like she had. She never lied.

'Really? You care for me? Not love, no? Not need? Because I think if you're honest with yourself, I would be somewhere on the list, but not the top. If I dropped out of your life, you wouldn't suffer, would you?'

'Are you leaving me, is that what you're saying?' Her heart sped up, and she knew what she wanted her answer to be. If he left now, she'd be screwed for going away, but that wasn't a reason to keep him with her.

'No!' The voice barked back, angry. 'You're still not listening Kate! You never hear me! I'm not leaving. You are though, you're constantly leaving. You dip in and out of my life like a side show. We're married Kate, that means something to me.'

'I come home every night Neil, if I'm not working. You knew the job I did when we met. It's demanding, but I'm still your wife.'

Neil sighed, a slow, desperate sounding sigh.

'No one's perfect Kate, God knows I'm not. I regret a lot of things. If you want to go on the trip, go. I can't stop you, I won't. I just want you to remember this conversation. Think about it when you're gone. I need you to get this Kate. You can't keep living like this. We can't.

I'll be home in the morning to take Jamie to school. When you get back, if you want me to go, I'll go. But you have to think about this. I think I already know the answer, but I'll give you the trip to give me an answer.'

'Neil, don't go, we need to sort this out! I don't want you driving when you're upset.' She sighed. 'I can't end our marriage over the phone.' The silence was deafening.

'But you do want to end things.' His voice was weak, flat. 'Is that what you're finally telling me.'

She sighed, holding the phone tight to her ear. 'I don't want to keep upsetting you,' she said honestly. 'Come home, let's talk. I can't go on this trip till things are settled.'

'They are,' Neil answered. 'I have my answer. I still want you to think about it when you're away, but I doubt distance will change things. I can't do this any more, it's not good for any of us. I get it, Kate. We tried. I'll see you tomorrow.'

Kate was about to ask where he was going to sleep when the line went dead. That was it, then. She'd done it. Ended them, over the phone in a five-minute call. She should be heartbroken, shouldn't she? Feel bereft? Want to call him back, beg him to come home. There was nothing. Nothing but relief, and huge, gut-wrenching guilt. She had broken up their family, and she felt freer than she had in years. It was done. She'd go on the trip, and deal with the aftermath when she got back. It was better for all of them, in the long term. Perhaps Neil would finally be happy again. She knew she would, even though looking her son in the face tomorrow morning would no doubt kill her. He was the casualty in their war, and she'd just fired the kill shot.

She looked around their home, at the schedules and pictures on the fridge. The photos on the walls, the lines drawn on the door frame that marked the journey of Jamie's growth. She knew one thing, whatever was going on with her and Neil, she had to be true to herself. Jamie was her priority, but she had to like herself as a person too. She knew what that meant. She knew that this choice was important, but she was used to making split second decisions and living with the consequences. Once she chose to do something, she saw it through. Just like her marriage. Fight or flight. She didn't run, she faced things head-on. What Neil did with her decision was up to him. It had been made, and no tour of duty was going to change something she should have done years ago. If Jamie hadn't come along, Kate knew that she and Neil would never have lasted. It hurt, but it was the right thing. Going away would help Neil to see that too.

She took a large calming sip of the wine and scrolled through her contacts before hitting dial. A familiar voice picked up the other line.

'Kate! Hey stranger, given it some thought?' Trevor said into her ear.

Kate smiled at her mentor's upbeat and hopeful voice. 'Yep, and I'm all in.'

3

COOPER

My throat felt like dry fire. I attempted a cough, but nothing came out, and I felt my heart race. I tried to lift up my head, but it felt as though it was stuck to the pillow. Raising my hand to touch my face, I felt a tug of pain. Looking at the back of my hand, I saw a butterfly drip stuck into it. Trying to focus my eyes, which felt like they had been taken out and dipped in sand, I saw a dim light in the corner of the room. I felt a warm presence on my other hand, and looked to see what was laid across it. My whole body felt fuzzy, with a dim undertone of throbbing pain. My hand, still resting on the bed, looked unnatural, and I realised that the extra fingers didn't belong to me. I squeezed gently, which was an achievement in itself. The fingers wrapped around mine squeezed back. My gritty eyes followed the fingers up the arm, and I realised a woman was asleep in the chair next to me. Even in sleep, she looked exhausted, pale blue scrubs encasing her lithe body. The hand holding mine had a wedding ring on it I noticed, and I felt a little pang of unexplained disappointment. Pushing the thought away, I tried to make my eyes focus on her again. She was pretty, little snuffles coming from her as she slept deeply. She had squeezed my hand back in reflex, unconsciously in sleep. I wanted to move my hand away, embarrassed by the contact, but I didn't move. She felt familiar, her touch soothing.

Looking around, I saw everyone was asleep, except for a couple of nurses milling around the area. It was then that I noticed what was missing: the noise. There was no gunfire, no explosions. All I could hear were the sounds of nature outside the tent. I think that this was more unnerving than being woken by the sounds of war, and I kept my ears open for any sound of impending danger. I felt so groggy, and my legs were numb. Trying to lift my head again, I pushed through the pain to look down at my body. Lifting the covers laid over me, I saw that I was naked. They must have cut my clothes off. I glanced across at the doctor in the chair. Had she seen me naked? I almost laughed out loud. The first time a woman had seen my dick in years, and I was unconscious and bleeding at the time. Very sexy. Go figure.

Pushing down the covers again, being careful not to move my hand from hers, I looked down at my legs. I half-expected to see two stumps, but there they were, although one of them looked like it was in a real mess, the whole thing encased in bandages. The shape was off, like someone had shaved off some ribbons of flesh. But I still had two legs, that was a good start. My torso was bandaged too, with a tube coming out of one side. Probably a drain, I realised. I had seen enough injured buddies to realise that a bomb blast ripped through your body like a hurricane, tearing organs, snapping bones, taking the very soul from a man. I was still here, so I would take it from there.

'Morning, Captain,' a soft voice said, thick with sleep. I lowered the covers quickly, aware that I had probably just been flashing the crown jewels. 'It's Kate. I'm glad you got some rest. You needed it.'

I looked across at her. She was stretching in the chair, hand still on mine, rubbing the sleep from her pretty almond eyes. 'I didn't see a thing, don't worry. How are you feeling?'

I cut her off before she could go into full bedside manner mode. 'My unit?'

'You don't remember?'

'Remember what?' I replied, my voice gruff, raspy. It came out harsher than I intended. I wasn't one for small talk at the best of times, and worry was spiking my adrenaline. The monitor beeped a little faster from somewhere behind my head.

Her face fell. 'The man you were carrying, he didn't make it. I'm s—'

I raised my drip hand at her. 'I know about Smithy, what about the others?'

She smiled a little then, relieved to have been asked another question. 'They are all out, safe and sound.'

I nodded, a wave of relief coursing over me. Then I remembered something.

'There was a boy, on the roof.' My voice pushed out the words in a croak. Her smile was dazzling this time.

'He's fine. Safe. You saved him.' She was looking at me like I was a hero. It was... new.

'Hightower okay?'

Kate laughed. 'He's good. Tried to take down half the staff to get to you. I'll make sure he knows you're awake. How's your pain?'

'Can't feel a thing.' She didn't look too pleased about that, but I brushed it off. 'When can I get back to duty?'

Her face fell, and she looked down at our hands. I pulled mine away then, and she let it go without a fight.

'Dr Trevor Tanner is going to come and talk to you soon, on his rounds.'

I grunted in annoyance. 'I'm not some idiot, missy. I just want to know when.'

She raised her chin at me then, her face hardening a little. 'First of all, I'm not "missy", I'm Dr Kate Harper. I'm an orthopaedic surgeon attached to your unit and several others, and as I said, Dr Tanner, my superior, is going to come and speak to you on rounds...' She checked her watch. '...Which started half an hour ago. I need to go, I'll come and check on you soon.'

She stood up and strode off haughtily. I laughed at her swagger. This one was a real ball buster, I could tell. I could have been nicer to her. The thought of her sleeping with her hand holding mine clouded my thoughts. I had no time for anything that wasn't getting back to my unit. I was Captain Cooper, not Mr Hearts and Flowers. She was a medic, she patched people like me up and sent them back out there. Still, winding her up gave me something. A distraction from being in this bed.

'Okay, Missy,' I shouted after her, chuckling. 'Don't get your knickers in a twist.'

I sniggered again as she made a 'humpf' sound, her nose pointing at the air furiously as she sped up her stomp. My whole body screamed at me for laughing, but it was so worth it.

* * *

Trevor was doing his rounds when she found him, and she could tell from his face that they had had a good night. A good night here was when they still had the same number alive as the day before. A great day was when there were no casualties at all, but sometimes the team was hard pushed to remember many days like that.

'Captain Cooper thinks he is hilarious. I'm just waiting for him to call me "toots" and slap me on the behind,' Kate said, still a little shocked at his reaction. She'd just spent the night holding his hand, thinking what a hero he was. *What was it with alphas and their bravado?* Trevor checked the vitals on his sleeping patient, and satisfied, made notes on his chart.

'So he's awake? That's amazing! How is he doing? How are his vitals?'

'He's stable, the chest drain is working well. I'm

still concerned about his leg though. He has limited blood flow to the area, and I'm worried about sepsis. I think the next couple of hours will be crucial.'

Trevor nodded sadly. 'So, he will probably lose the leg, if we try to keep him alive.' He rubbed at his temples. 'Not told him any of this, have you?'

Kate shook her head. 'I told him you would explain on this morning's ward round. I wanted to go through everything again, monitor him closely for as long as we safely can before we make a decision.'

Trevor looked at her, his face unreadable. 'It may not be our decision, it's up to him.'

Kate looked nonplussed. 'The evac chopper is coming in two days. At present, he's too unstable to move. We need to get him home then, leg or no leg. A decision between losing a limb and dying is not a great thing to have thrust at you, granted – but he wants to live, surely?'

Trevor placed the chart at the foot of the bed and started to walk towards the next patient, issuing medication instructions to the nurse as he walked.

'Kate,' he began in a tone he might have used to tell his child that Father Christmas wasn't real. 'I have worked on men like Captain Cooper since this whole nightmare started. These are army men to the core. Sometimes going home means no family, no buddies, no job, and a lifetime of relying on other people. They are proud, and sometimes, to them, the reality is worse than death. Don't take anything for granted when it comes to patient wishes.'

Kate ran her fingers through her hair, suddenly feeling tired all over again. He'd never asked anything about himself, his injuries. Whether he was going to live through this. He'd only asked about returning to his team. His sudden macho turnaround made sense now. He was fearful for his career, and she understood that. Trying to keep her career on track hadn't been life or death, but she had felt torn about not being able to do it, or do it well. Hell, if she didn't have Jamie to go home to and a marriage breakdown to navigate, she would already have signed up for another tour. She couldn't imagine not being a doctor. It was part of her.

'Cooper knows that. Better than most, probably. Let's see what happens. If we can head off the sepsis, we might not have to cross that bridge.'

'Understood.'

* * *

'So what you're saying, Doc, is that I'm screwed.' Captain Cooper was sat up in bed now, the drain poking out from his side. The internal bleeding had been dealt with, his chest now free from shrapnel. All his organs were intact, and the tears in his body had been sewn up, the bleeding stopped.

Trevor pulled a chair across to sit near his bedside. 'Your left leg is bad, Captain. You're starting to show signs of severe infection, and we feel that a below knee amputation is needed. Your chest injuries will take substantial time to heal, and your right leg has been injured by shrapnel from the bomb too. Returning to your unit is out of the question, at least for now. You have a place on the chopper, but the next few hours will decide whether you are fit enough to make the journey back to the UK.'

Captain Cooper sat motionless in the bed, his mind obviously working overtime as he processed the information. Kate stood behind Trevor, watching Cooper with interest. She couldn't imagine having to make a decision like this. The consent to surgery papers in her hand felt heavy, weighted with their implication.

'And when do you need an answer?' Cooper said flatly, not looking at Trevor, but directly at Kate. She blushed under his intent gaze and felt pathetic that her body responded to the pull of attraction she felt to this man at such a time. Trevor pulled a marker pen out of his top pocket, and lifting the covers, made a mark on the area of skin just poking out from the top of the bandages.

'We need to monitor you. This will tell us if the antibiotics are working – we need to watch out for any colour changes above this line on your leg. We have to make a decision tonight, and I would highly recommend that you have the surgery Captain, and be on that chopper when it leaves.'

Kate looked away from the captain's face, feeling his gaze on her again. She didn't trust her own face not to betray her emotions. A deep voice broke the silence of the machines beeping in the room.

'I withhold consent.'

Kate snapped her head towards the voice. Cooper looked determined, resigned to his decision and angry, as though he was daring them to challenge him. Her heart sank.

'Captain, you do realise that—'

'Yes, Missy. I realise what I am saying, and I withhold consent. You can't take my leg.'

'You have to live, you can live without a leg. With modern-day medical advances, you can still live a good life. It's not over for you.' She was speaking too much, going against her training, but she wanted him to have the facts. That was her job, to lay out the options. She had no personal stake in this, even though everything in her was screaming that she wanted him to live. What was the point if not? Of meeting him, of the boy being saved, just for another life to be wasted in its place?

'I withhold consent. You can keep your medical advances.'

Kate opened her mouth to argue, moving closer to the bed, but Trevor stood up to stop her.

'Captain, that is your decision, but let's see what happens over the next few hours, okay? Think it over, we realise it's a huge decision to make.'

The captain snorted. 'No shit, Doc. I won't change my mind.'

Trevor nodded, an almost imperceptive movement. 'Kate, keep me updated.' He left the area to tend to other patients.

The captain looked at her again, and she felt a flush creep across her skin as his eyes ran over her body. For a nude man, he had the undressing people with your eyes thing nailed. She was the one who felt naked, exposed in front of him.

'I know you don't get it, but this *is* my life. Without it, there's not much to stay alive for.'

'I get it more than you think,' she sighed. 'But we are not there yet. The medication could still turn things around.' She put the papers down at the side of his bed. 'Is there anyone I can call for you?'

'Nope, everyone's already here.' Cooper crossed his arms gently, his pale face wincing at the pain of his movements. Which meant he was getting worse, if the injuries were making themselves known even over the pain meds. She checked his morphine drip as his eyes followed her movements. He was looking sicker and sicker as time passed, and she knew he must feel it.

'So,' he rasped. 'Your husband serve too?'

The mention of a husband had her head turning towards him.

'No, he's back home, with my son.'

Cooper nodded, his jaw tightening. 'What does he think of you being out here, in all this?'

'Well,' she checked the monitors again and sagged down into the chair she'd slept in. 'My son is still little and believes in superheroes, so he thinks I'm pretty cool. Like Captain America or something.'

'Wonderwoman,' Cooper added. 'What about your husband?'

The smile dropped from her lips. 'Well, he's my soon to be ex-husband, so he's not so keen about...' She waved a hand around the tent. '...all this. He thinks I ran away.'

'Did you?' When she met his green eyes, she saw no judgement.

She laughed a little, despite herself. 'No. Yes. A little bit. I wanted to come and help, do something. Learn new skills, I guess, but I can't say that I wasn't glad to come out here.'

'How long you been married?'

'Too long,' was all she would allow herself to say. 'We had Jamie by accident, really. It seemed like the natural thing to do.'

'Jamie's your son?'

'Yeah.' She pulled out her phone, showed him her screensaver of him in his football kit.

'Cute kid.'

'What about you?'

His dark brows knitted together. 'What about me?'

'What do you have back home?' His expression started to close off, and she rushed to fill the awkward pause. 'I mean, when you're not protecting the world and saving kids on rooftops.'

'I never really did the traditional way of living,' he tried to shrug but his whole body tensed from the movement. 'I have my unit, and that's more than enough.'

They stared at each other for a long time, but it wasn't awkward. He looked like he was trying to figure her out just as she was him. 'What if you need the surgery?'

His lips pursed. 'I won't.' She felt like she should say more, tell him how precarious his condition was, but he spoke first. 'Tell me, if you couldn't be a doctor, what would you do? How would you spend your life?'

Kate's mind flashed to an image of Jamie, at home with Neil, the man she had flown to a warzone to get some space from, and she closed her mouth, tensing her jaw. 'I honestly don't know,' she murmured. 'I love my son, but—'

'You don't really like the traditional way either.'

'I guess we're similar in that way.'

'Guess we are.' His smile, when it came, lit his pale face up. 'My life is here, I have no plan B.'

Kate thought of his wallet, bearing no pictures of home or family. There wouldn't be anyone flying a banner for the captain when he touched down on the tarmac. He needed to get through this. She pushed the thought away, taking a breath.

'Well Captain—'

'Coop, please. We've held hands, and I'm pretty sure you've seen me naked.'

She nodded, the corners of her mouth lifting up. 'We're not at plan B, Coop. Get some rest.'

He relaxed a little, offering her a cheeky half-smile as he rested back against his pillows.

'Maybe just for a minute,' he winced as he adjusted himself into a better position. 'Feel like I've been hit by a damn truck.'

Kate waited till he was asleep, his breathing even, before she reached for his hand again. Resolving that while he was here, he would have someone. Her.

* * *

Kate was sleeping in her cot when she was shaken awake by a frantic nurse. 'Dr Harper, Cooper is crashing.' Kate leapt from her bed, still fully dressed in her scrubs and raced to the tent with the nurse hot on her heels. 'How long has he been down?' she shouted over her shoulder.

'Less than two minutes, I came straight here.'

'Where's Trevor?' Kate shouted, racing across the dust for the entrance to the tent, ignoring the burn of the sand in her eyes from the grit her frantic feet were kicking up.

'He's in surgery, we had another IED casualty come in an hour ago.'

'Shit,' Kate said. 'Fuck!' Racing across to the captain, she saw doctors and nurses running around.

Whipping back the covers, she saw what she had feared and she sent up a curse to the almighty. His infection had taken hold with a vengeance, the discoloured skin now seeping well past Trevor's pen line.

'Okay, let's run the code. Charge to 300.' Kate grabbed the paddles, hands shaking. 'Now guys, let's go, his organs are failing! Someone should have called me sooner!'

'We were checking him,' the nurse protested. 'He kept refusing to let us check!'

Damn it. I withhold consent. She could hear his voice in her head as she fought to bring him back.

The machine bleeped its readiness. 'Clear!' she shouted, shocking the captain's chest. She checked the monitor again. 'No output, charge to 350.' She turned, wide-eyed to the side table. 'Did he sign the papers? The consent papers, did he sign them?'

'No,' the nurse confirmed. 'He was asleep, but we operate, right? We need to take the leg to save him.'

It was different here. Not everyone was in shape to give consent, and when medical intervention was needed it was done. To save the patient. 'He didn't want this, I need Trevor. Clear!'

The 350 charge jolted his body.

Nurse Abby looked at Kate. 'Kate, he refused amputation verbally only. He didn't sign papers to withhold consent. Protocol is we save him, given that he's not in a position to sign either way. He's been down for three minutes, and unless we amputate, his body will continue to shut down. I think we need to make a call.' The monitors continued their music, the beep of a man circling the drain.

Kate stood, paddles in hand, trying to think. 'Have you called Trevor?'

'He's in surgery, he can't come.'

'Did he sign a DNR?' Kate asked frantically, trying to justify the decision she knew she wanted to take. 'Did he put anything in writing?'

Abby shook her head. 'No. We could wait for Trevor, he's being told right now but that might be too late. Kate! We need to prep for amputation!'

Medic Jones came running in, radio in hand. 'Trevor made the call – if no papers were signed, we proceed as normal.'

'Shit. Okay, okay. Thanks.' Trevor was there when he said he didn't want the operation. He was her superior. It came down to him, but she would have to be the one to do it. To look him in the eye after. He might never get back to his unit. Active duty was far harder for amputees. He wouldn't be the captain he loved being after this. Kate looked at the man on the bed, and thought of the boy on the roof. If Cooper died, what would be the point in any of this? Would she want Jamie's survival to mean another life lost, if her child had been on that rooftop? Life was made of split-second decisions, and Kate had made enough to know that she would rather choose fast and live with the fallout. The thought of letting him die felt wrong. She just knew that the world still had plans for this soldier, even if he didn't realise it yet. She would live with her decision. If the captain couldn't deal with it, then that was his choice. He could die, just not today, and not on her watch. She had to follow orders.

'Patients change their mind. Do you want to be responsible for a death that could have been prevented? Kate, please – charge!' Kate looked at the nurse, feeling the sweat drip down her spine inside her scrubs. She was terrified, but she just couldn't let him go out like this. Her mind was set. Abby looked at her and the others around them, and shaking her head, she ordered another charge.

The beeping noise told Kate the unit was ready.

'Clear!' she shouted, shocking the captain again. His body jerked and this time, his eyes fluttered. A flash of green she thought she might never see again. She looked desperately at the monitor. Nothing. Nothing on the screen but a line, and a beep heralding the call of the end. Nothing, nothing, then a beat, beat,

beat. The pixels on the screen danced across, levelling into a pattern. The prettiest pattern Dr Harper had ever seen.

'We have him back,' she said, putting the paddles away. 'Gown me up,' she ordered.

'I need a bone saw and a ten blade, now.'

Abby nodded, running to the sterile equipment store and grappling for implements with sure hands. Kate snipped away the bandages, another nurse prepped the surgical field, and a doctor worked on anaesthetising the captain.

Moments later, someone passed the blade to her. She took a deep breath, looking at Cooper's unconscious face, and made the first cut.

Please forgive me.

4

COOPER

I dreamt I was running across the dust, bullets whizzing past my ear as I raced for shelter, my gun tight to my side. The radio was buzzing in my jacket, shouting my name. 'Cooper, Cooper, come in.'

Around me, the crumbling buildings fell apart, destroyed by shells and the anger of men. The ground was unsafe, potholes forming before my eyes, rocks shooting up like newly erected buildings. The radio voice kept insisting I move. Keep moving, don't stop, or you'll be no more.

I kept running, boots clicking on stones and rubble, sinking into puddles of blood, pieces of the buildings around me laying at my head like rose petals as I literally ran for my life. The noise in the radio changed. This one was female, strong, anguished. Familiar somehow, but he couldn't summon up a face to match the voice in his head.

'Cooper, you have to fight. Cooper, you have to live. Wake up, Cooper, wake up...'

I jumped as a pain shot through my lower body. My eyes snapped open, and I realised I was in the same tent, the same bed. It had been a nightmare. I could feel the sweat dripping down my forehead, I was drenched. The bed sheets felt wet, sticky to the touch. I flexed my fingers, testing out how my body was holding up. My right hand felt heavy, and I could feel warm, soft skin against mine. I smiled despite myself, and opening my eyes, saw Kate asleep in the chair, her hand wrapped around mine. She'd stayed with me again. This angel in the dust. It made me wonder what sort of man she was splitting up from back home. Whether I would measure up. Where that thought had even come from. I didn't exactly date, nor feel the need to. Something about her made me think of more than war. *Must be the meds.* Still, I took a moment to savour the warm fuzzies I felt at waking up again with this woman holding my hand. My whole body felt sluggish, achy and my legs were killing me, a dull but insistent pain running through them. I squeezed her hand, running my fingers along her wedding band. I wonder what sort of guy had this woman's heart, even for a short time. Another doctor, probably, as driven and stubborn as her. She squeezed my hand back, and when I looked at her, her blue eyes were looking straight into mine.

'Morning, Missy,' I said weakly, my voice coming out as a rasp. 'Did I oversleep?'

She didn't acknowledge my attempt at humour, but I clocked the relief on her pretty face. The blood froze in my veins when I realised what that meant.

'This is it then, yeah?' I asked. 'How long have I got?'

She leaned forward, the dark circles under her eyes giving her a haunted look under the dimmed strip lighting in the tent. 'Your organs started to shut down, and your heart stopped.'

I frowned. 'So how am I talking to you?'

Kate looked away from me, and I tried to sit up. She placed her other hand on my chest, stilling me.

'No, please, don't try to move.'

I looked at her again, and I knew. I reached for the sheet and whipped it back. She said nothing, standing and helping me to pull the cover down slowly. My right leg was still bandaged up, my toes poking out of the end, but my left leg looked different. My brain seemed to short out a second, and I wiggled my toes.

Wiggled them again. My brain told me that I had just wiggled ten toes, but my eyes told me different. On my left leg, where my toes should have been, there was just the expanse of the bed. My leg was bandaged, and stopped just below where my knee should be. I became aware of a high-pitched gurgle, an unholy sound, and I looked from my legs to Kate and then around the room, searching for the source of the noise.

Kate touched my face, cupping my cheeks between her hands, and turned me to face her. 'I am so sorry, Captain. I am so sorry. You need to stay calm; your stitches are still fresh.'

It was then that I realised that the noise was coming from me, but I still couldn't stop it. It was like my soul was ripping itself in two, and I laid back against the covers as my head swam.

Looking down at my legs again, I closed my eyes tight.

'Put the cover back,' I begged. Kate wrapped me up again, checking the monitor, her face a mask of stricken pain.

'Do you need more pain relief?' she asked softly. I nodded, and she turned to the fluid bag my IV drip was connected to.

I looked up at the ceiling, not wanting to catch

sight of my broken body under the sheets. *I didn't want this.*

Kate took a seat in the chair beside me, and I turned my head to look at her. Her face soothed me, and I didn't have the strength to unpick at the whys and wherefores in that moment. Too much hurt, so I focused on what didn't. What helped keep me from thrashing around in this bed, breaking everything I could get my hands on.

'You were crashing, so we had to make a call. You didn't make it, we had to revive you twice. I had no choice; you must know that. I didn't want to—'

I felt as though she had slapped me. 'You took my leg?' I said gruffly. 'You did this to me?'

I watched tears spring into her eyes, and she swallowed hard, blinking rapidly. A single tear escaped from her eye and ran down her cheek, and she wiped at it quickly, erasing the evidence.

'Yes, I operated.'

I nodded. The drugs started to kick in again, the pain in my body numbing. I didn't try to fight the sleep that was coming, it felt like sweet oblivion was sweeping in to take me away, and I welcomed it. I whispered something, my voice giving out, and Kate leaned closer, her ear hovering over my mouth. I caught the scent of her perfume in my nostrils, and I felt a twitch in my lower body. I would have laughed at the inappropriateness of it all, but I couldn't muster the energy. *I definitely didn't measure up now. Not that it mattered any more.*

'What did you say?' she asked. She went to fill a cup with water and put the straw near my mouth. I took a sip and felt the coolness of the water drifting down my throat. I tried again to spit out the words that were screaming inside my brain like a pinball in an arcade machine.

'You should have let me die,' I breathed, and sleep took me under.

5

'We followed protocol, Kate. He might not see that now, but no papers were signed. We have to make these calls in the field all the time. If we have to get paperwork signed for everything we did, half the soldiers here wouldn't make it. It's not like back home, it was an emergent situation. He expressed it verbally, but the situation worsened and we could no longer ask him his wishes. It's on me. I'll tell him it was my call.'

'No,' Kate felt numb, but she didn't need anyone to take the rap for her. 'He needs a doctor he can trust, and I'm not that person any more. Don't tell him. There's no point. I made the cut, either way.' She couldn't regret her decision. She wouldn't. She'd followed orders, saved a life. There was no point in regret, not here. It was done, and she would live with it. He'd live – and hate her forever. It was that point that bothered her more than anything else. It was irritational. Unprofessional, but unshakable from her thoughts. She couldn't explain why this man meant so much to her, at this point in time and place. What it meant. Yet she couldn't bear to think of him just slipping away, somehow. She knew in her gut that he wasn't done. Maybe one day he would see that too, and hate her a little less. She would be home in mere weeks, and she would be some woman, part of a bad memory in his head. *At least he will be alive*; she comforted herself with that thought as she sat there. After the debrief, when she had a break in duties, she gravitated back to him.

Cooper hadn't spoken again, he was still sleeping off the meds. She had stayed at his bedside all night, checking his vitals, and now she had a crick in her neck and a heavy weight deep in the pit of her stomach. She had watched him sleep fitfully, his temperature spiking as his body fought off the remnants of the infection. Around five that morning, he had turned the corner, his vitals stabilising. Taking his leg had saved his life, and Kate was so relieved she could cry. His words, however, would haunt her for the rest of her days, and she wasn't looking forward to facing him once he woke up. She wondered whether he would ever be thankful for what she did, given time. Wished she could be around to see how he was down the line.

For now, she could make sure he wasn't alone. She got up when her phone rang. Seeing her husband's name flash up on her screen, she sighed. Thinking about Neil was the last thing she needed right now, but he was back home, holding the fort with their son. After ending things, she owed him to at least pick up.

'Hello?' Cooper was still out, and a nurse was nearby. She walked towards her bed, wishing that the day was over already.

6

Abby came into the small office area off the ward, to see Kate surrounded by various charts and files.

'He got you doing paperwork?'

'Yep,' she said with a sigh. 'I don't mind.' She didn't voice the fact that they were quiet today. Saying things like that tended to trigger things in the medical profession. It was an unspoken code that all medics followed. Tempting fate was never a good move. 'Keeps me busy.'

Abby nodded to the countertop, clicking on the kettle. 'Coffee?'

Kate looked at the desk next to her, where an assortment of dirty cups littered the surfaces. 'Sure, one more can't hurt. I won't sleep anyway. You might need a mug though. I'll help.' She got to work, dumping all the crockery into the sink and washing them. She passed two mugs to Abby, who was busy munching away on a cereal bar like a starving squirrel. 'How is he?'

Abby's eyes sparked with recognition. Her nurse friend had seen her sitting with Cooper enough to know who she was asking about. She'd tried to keep her distance, as much as she could, sensing that her face might not be the one he'd want to see when his emerald green eyes opened. 'He's stable, but still out. He's hopefully going to be weaned off the meds a bit tonight, we'll see how he feels then. The operation worked though, signs of sepsis are gone.'

Kate felt her heart beat, as though it had taken a misstep. 'Drain? Any signs of wound infection, tissue necrosis? Urine output?'

Abby took the barrage of questions in her stride. 'Drain should be out tomorrow, no infection or necrosis. The site looks good Kate, you did a good job. Urine output is low, but he was a little dehydrated from the field anyway. We're still pushing fluids.'

Kate ran through the knowledge in her head, looking for anything she missed. Abby tapped her on the arm.

'Kate, you didn't miss anything. He made it. He will make it. You did good.'

Kate didn't hear the praise. She just thought about what it would take to get him to see that living was worth it. She had to make him understand, even though she wasn't entirely sure herself what her reasons were. She thought of her conversation with Neil earlier. Yet again, he had called to moan about how much he had to do: the washing, Jamie, work. He was mad at her for going. For ending things and leaving him in limbo... It hung in the air between them. She had apologised, as she always did; she apologised for choosing to keep chasing her own career. Hurt, Neil was focusing on what she'd left him with. Carrying the baby, so to speak. He'd even used the phrase single parent, and she'd bitten her tongue so she didn't point out that this is what they were now, no matter what continent she was on. Jamie was looked after by his own father, who helped make him, but this of course went unsaid, as usual. She often wondered what the world would look like if humans were like seahorses, and the men had to carry babies through to birth. Odds on, humanity would grind to a shuddering halt.

'Has he been awake at all?'

Abby shook her head, making the coffees for them both. 'Nope, thankfully. He needs the rest. Does his family know? I haven't checked his file yet for contact details.'

Kate shook her head. 'No, he has no one.'

Abby pursed her lips. 'Jesus. Well, at least you've been there for him.'

Kate took a sip of her own drink, feeling the jolt of caffeine top up her already wired body.

'Thanks,' she said, heading back over to the piles of paper she still had to wade through. 'I hope he sees it that way, eventually.'

'He's here, Kate. He has a chance.' Abby left, leaving her alone with the piles and piles of charting, and her thoughts of everything she had to face in the next few weeks.

* * *

Kate was back in her bunk, sleeping off the exhaustion and taut limbs that a day full of paperwork and segregating her life with Neil in her head had brought on, when her phone beeped. She jerked awake, reaching for the handset. Abby had messaged an emoji of a pair of eyes, with the words 'he's awake...' Kate sprang from her bed. She shoved a clean pair of scrubs on, dressing quickly and quietly as others slept and relaxed around her. She turned her phone to silent, not wanting it to go off while she was in the medical tent. It was late, and the patients would be sleeping. She entered the tent. Abby had her back to her, bent over her desk, but she waved her hand towards Cooper's bed. Kate took a breath and looked around. There were only three patients in the beds, the others having been patched up or medevacked home. Kate walked over to the captain's bed, cautious that she might make him feel worse, but she needed to see him. Another man in her life that she was disappointing. She neared the foot of the bed, and he turned his head to face her. He had been awake a while by the looks, seemingly staring at the wall. Kate felt a jolt as he looked straight into her eyes. He looked pale and exhausted, his jaw set like a block of stone. The green of his eyes wasn't diminished though, and she had a flashback to the day he came in. The look in them was very different today. There was nothing in them but hate, reflected straight back at her.

Kate stopped walking, looking across at the chair at the side of the bed.

'Do you mind if I sit?'

He didn't say anything at first, he just pinned her with those green eyes. He was acting like he was chewing his tongue off. She wondered if he was suffering. She took a step closer to the chair.

'Are you in pain?' She went to reach for his chart. 'I can ask Abby to give you some pain relief, I just need to check—'

'Don't touch my chart. I don't want you anywhere near me.'

Kate's hand stilled. 'I understand you're upset, but I just came to check on you.'

He chuckled under his breath. 'Check you haven't got a dead man on your hands you mean. You might still have, so I hope you kept my leg. I would like to be buried whole.'

'Captain, I—'

'I'm not interested in anything you have to say, Doc. I should be suing you for not following my orders. I never asked you to save me. In fact, I pretty much insisted that you do the opposite.'

Kate noticed that Abby had stood up and was making her way over, a panicked look on her face.

'Kate,' she whispered. 'Everything okay?'

Cooper growled. 'Great, sure. The Doc was just leaving.'

'Cooper, I—'

'Leave!' he growled, lifting himself up off the covers. He started coughing, a hand flying to his chest. His monitor beeped faster. Abby rushed to his bedside, helping him to sit up a little.

'Kate, you should go. Now.'

Kate looked at them both, Cooper still coughing and wincing in pain, and turned on her heel. She didn't stop till she was back in her bunk, which was when the tears started to flow. He hated her. She'd destroyed another man's life by trying to do the right thing. And the worst of it was, she felt alone again.

* * *

The next day, Kate was on desk duties again, but she and Trevor both knew that it couldn't last. There were too many things to do, they were too busy to be able to afford a doctor not seeing to the patients. It was thankfully quiet, but the other doctors would be feeling the strain soon. She would have to go back to the tent, work on patients. Finish what she came here to do. Trevor had insisted again on wanting to tell Cooper that he had made the call on his treatment, but Kate shut him down. He was lead surgeon, he didn't need the wrath of the captain. It wouldn't make him hate Kate any less. She would just bear it, do her job and stay out of his way till his ride home came. After today, he would never have to see her again.

Kate had wanted to make him see that he was worth saving, and that he could still have a life. It wasn't the end. She knew from her job that people coped, adapted. He could too. Anyone who would be brave enough to walk into battle and be responsible for the people under his command must surely see the preciousness of life, and the necessity to survive.

Kate was just standing up to go to the medical bay when her phone rang. She pulled it out of her pocket and pulled a face, walking into the corridor. Trevor was coming her way, and her gut clenched.

'Neil, it's not a good time. Is everything okay?'

She winced as she heard the sound of sirens and machinery in her ear, and her husband's panicked voice stopped her in her tracks.

'Kate, Kate, don't hang up! It's Jamie, th-there's been an accident. It's bad Kate, really bad. So much blood... I am so sorry.' Neil started to cry down the phone, a wet whimpering sound. She cupped the phone to her ear, her legs falling out from under her. Trevor, aware something was wrong, appeared at her side, lowering her to the tent floor.

'Kate,' he said in a tone of voice she had never heard from him before. 'Kate, what's wrong?'

She willed her mouth to open, to form words, but all that came out was a whispered 'Jamie?'

Trevor took the phone from her, and she let him, her arm flopping to her lap.

'Neil, it's Trevor. What's happened?'

Kate looked up at Trevor, trying to decipher the news from his face. Trevor went pale, and she whimpered. *'Jamie, my poor Jamie, no, no, no...'*

Trevor said something into the phone and ended the call. He knelt down, pushing the phone into her hands.

'Kate, get up. Jamie is alive.'

Kate's head snapped up to look at him then, and the fog that surrounded her body lifted, leaving the adrenaline free to course through her veins. She stood up, gripping her mobile for dear life. Trevor put his hands on her shoulders and forced her to look at him.

'Kate, listen, they've been in a car accident. Jamie needs you, okay?' Kate felt the words wash over her as Trevor ran his fingers down her shoulders. 'The chopper will be here in a few hours, and you need to be on it. Go get your stuff. I'll sort things here.'

Kate looked at Trevor, numb. 'Kate,' he tried again. 'Get packed up, that's an order.'

Kate snapped back into reality and ran to her bunk. Three hours later, though it felt more like three months, Kate was being strapped into her seat by a medic, who was shouting instructions at his colleagues. They loaded a soldier onto the chopper, sedated for the journey home. One was already loaded, next to where she was sitting. Kate looked across to the man strapped to a gurney and noticed that it was Captain Cooper. Of course. This was the flight he was going to take if he was stable enough. She couldn't help thinking that he could have been on the same flight in a box, had she not interfered, and she wondered if he would make that connection for himself. Whether it would make a difference to him. Get him to rethink whether he was glad to be alive or not.

Meanwhile her boy was hurt, miles away from her. Maybe it was karma. She'd taken away what Cooper loved with a twist of a scalpel. Maybe someone up there had sought to balance the scales, taking the thing she loved the most. She'd been here, in the dirt, ending a soldier's career, and her son had been hurt. Left unprotected. She couldn't bear it. She'd been dreading leaving this place, escaping from her failed marriage. Now, her failure was hitching a ride home with her. She looked across at him more closely. The thought of him being there both terrified her and comforted her.

His eyelids were fluttering in sleep, but his colour was better. Kate checked his stats on the monitor next to him. He was stable, and he was looking good. He wasn't even sedated, but she supposed that this was more down to his stubborn attitude than his medical condition. The chopper started to get ready for take-off, and she looked out of the window at the place she had called home for the past couple of months: a few tents in the desert, and days ago she would gladly have stayed another ten years than face what she was coming home to. They hadn't been able to get Neil back on the phone, and Kate feared the worst. Her boy needed her, and she had left him to come here, to this warzone, where men killed each other daily, snuffing out life wherever they found it. What kind of mother does that, she asked herself for the millionth time since she got the call. Jamie needed her, and she prayed to God that he was still alive. A god she hadn't seen much evidence of lately. She prayed silently. *Save my boy, please, save my boy. If you save him, I promise, I will put him first for as long as I live.*

She hadn't cried yet, but she knew it was coming. Her tear ducts weren't functioning, not listening to the brain's command to release some of the pent-up grief, worry, anger and chest-crushing fear that invaded every nerve ending of her body. All she felt was a constant stinging, a never-ending pain in her eyes, in her head. She wanted to gouge her eyes out, to stop the pain, but she concentrated on slowing her breathing instead. In, out. In, out. Her heart had not stopped racing and she was feeling light-headed.

She had to get it together. A sob erupted from her and she tried to squash it down, but more came, till she was racked with them, loud throaty sobs that stung her bone-dry eyes to the quick, that made her heart stab with pain. The medics sat nearby looked at her with concern, but knew well enough to leave her be. Nothing could be done to make her feel better, and they had work to do, with the sleeping heroes surrounding them. The sobs kept coming, and Kate was panicking, her breath getting shallower with every gasp. She started fumbling with her seatbelt, desperate to get up, get away. The medic nearest to her started to shout at her, telling her to stay buckled, stay down. At take-off, anything could happen, she needed to stay the hell down. She ignored him, focusing only on the monster of panic that sat on her back, weighing her down, till she heard a strong voice close to her.

'Sit down,' it said. She looked across at the medic, and he was busy talking to the pilot, the headset buzzing with their concerned voices in her ear. She ripped off her headset and heard the voice again, louder this time. 'Sit down and shut up, Doc.' She looked around her, desperate to find the source of the voice. *Was she losing her mind?*

Something brushed against her leg, pushing it down as she half-sat, half-stood, wrestling against her seatbelt restraints. She grabbed at the hand, and it closed tightly around her fingers. Cooper was looking right at her, a mixture of pain and concern etched on his features. She was blacking out, her breath rushing in and out of her too fast to help her stricken body. He squeezed her hand and pushed her back down into her seat. She gave up and sank down into the chair, gripping his fingers tight in hers.

'Look at me,' he demanded, his voice dry and husky. She looked at him then, his eyes immediately shooting through her body, pinning her in place. *Those eyes,* she thought to herself randomly. *I saved those eyes, and now they hate me. They hate me, and my son is probably dead.* Her vision started to dim a little, a tunnel of black appearing around the edges of her vision.

'Look at me!' the voice commanded, and she locked onto those eyes again. Cooper gave a little smile, so quick she debated whether it had really been there.

'Slow down. Concentrate on my voice, okay? Calm down. Breathe, just breathe. In,' he said, doing it with her. 'Out,' he said, pushing out a slow breath, wincing at the pain he was obviously feeling.

Kate concentrated on those eyes, and the ins and outs of her breathing, as it slowed down. The fear, like a boa constrictor around her throat, slithered looser, before slinking off to another poor mortal. She lined up her breathing with his, focusing on those pools of colour in his beautiful, pale, scratched face, and she felt a little snatch of peace. She went to move her hand away, a little embarrassed that the man who hated her was her saviour, but he gripped her tighter, not giving her an inch to wriggle away.

'Just...' he started, struggling with his next words. 'Just stay, okay? I'm here. I don't know what's wrong, but I'm here.'

She looked at the man on the gurney in front of her. Broken, battered, bruised, angry. She thought him, in that instance of time, the most exquisite thing she had ever seen. The strongest man she had ever known, and the thought was her undoing. Silent tears ran down her cheeks as she brought her hand to meet the other, sandwiching Cooper's strong warm one between them.

'I'm so sorry, I am so sorry, it's my fault, it's all my fault,' she said, rambling softly. She lowered her head and kissed the back of his hand, a hot tear dropping onto the skin, making the hairs stand on end. He said nothing, just ran his thumb over her fingers, holding hers fast, an anchor holding her into this moment. She lay back on the seat, exhausted now, and started to close her eyes. Every time she opened them it felt as though her corneas were being sliced with razor blades, so she kept them closed, focusing on the sound of the chopper blades and the feel of his steadying hand between hers. 'I think my son is dead,' she whispered. The hand squeezed tighter, and the tears kept flowing, silently running down onto her clothes, and their entwined hands.

* * *

Hours later, Captain Thomas Cooper woke to the sound of the medic readying his gurney for moving. The chopper was still, and Coop could hear trucks nearby, people milling around the hangar. He looked across, but the seat was empty. His hand, still wet from her tears, was placed at the side of his body on the bed and as he flexed it, he felt something in his palm. Lifting his hand, he saw a piece of paper, ripped out of a notepad, the clumsy way it was torn causing a jagged edge, softer than the harder, neater edges. He recognised the handwriting from the walls of the hospital, from the notes written on chalk boards and white boards around the tent he had been housed in. He unfolded it fully, ignoring the medics milling around him, the groans of his comrades as they were moved gently, one by one. The note read:

Thank you. I don't deserve your kindness, but I will never forget it. Now you need to do something for yourself, you need to live. You need to fight; this is not the end for you. Please, for the man you are, for the boy on the roof, for me, fight. Make this mean something.
  Kate

Cooper refolded the note carefully, holding it tight. *Make this mean something.* She'd been in bits on the chopper. The unflappable, gorgeous woman who'd taken his leg had near passed out in front of him. Stilled only by his hand, his words. As if his touch soothed her like she had him. He'd expected to wake up with her hand in his. Realised he missed it. Wanted it back. She sounded so desperate in her note, begging him to live. To fight. And that just pissed him right off, because before he'd read her words, he had no intention of trying. When the medic came back to move him, he looked at him enquiringly. 'The doctor who was here, where did she go?'

The medic, a young lad who looked like he had not slept in months, looked at him wearily.

'She went home, Captain. Family emergency.' *I think my son is dead.* That's why she was on that chopper. He thought of the boy on the rooftop. Her words to him after. What was it she said? Something about hoping a hero like him would be there if her boy needed one.

Cooper nodded. 'Where's home?' he asked.

The medic shrugged. 'No idea, man. You ready to go?'

Cooper sighed. 'Sure, nothing else to do, have I? And it's Captain to you.'

The medic blushed. 'Sorry, Captain. Roger that.'

7

Kate thanked the taxi driver and heaved herself out of the car, her duffle bag dragging along behind her. The night was still, and warm and she found herself grateful for the coverage of darkness. Everything was so familiar to her, yet so alien, different. She reached into the rockery, picking up the fake stone hide-a-key to let herself into her home. She had been surprised that Neil's car wasn't there when she first pulled up, but then she remembered. The accident. Their son had been cut out of their car. It was now lying in some police impound lot, or a scrap yard somewhere, waiting to be dealt with. She never wanted to see it again.

The hallway was in darkness, and she called for

Neil. His keys weren't on the hook, and there was no noise coming from the living room. He must have gone straight to bed. To get some rest. He was fine, but in shock. The doctor had advised him to rest up. She would still have been at the hospital too, but they had forced her to go home, get changed and sleep. Jamie would be in surgery for hours, and then recovery. She couldn't do anything, and she knew her presence there was distracting the staff. She needed them to concentrate on saving her son. She looked into the lounge, but it was empty. There was a plate on the coffee table, a piece of toast crust sitting on it. Remnants of jam sat on the plate, congealed. Jamie's Lego beaker was placed next to it, no doubt once containing milk. She imagined Jamie sitting there earlier in the day, eating his breakfast and watching cartoons. Probably leaving sticky jam fingers and toast crumbs on his clean, navy uniform. A boy on his way to school, and now fighting for his life. She left the crockery where it was, she couldn't bear to alter anything her son had touched.

'Neil?' she called. No answer. She sat on the bottom step, dropping her kit bag and unlaced her boots, dumping them on the hall floor. She pulled off her thick socks, her bare feet feeling odd against the plush carpeting as she took the stairs one by one.

'We can go back in a few hours, together. At least

we have my car in the garage, we can get around still.' She rounded the top of the stairs and pushed open their bedroom door.

'Did you get a taxi home?' she asked, looking at the bed. It was unmade, the pillows tousled, the sheets flipped back. It was empty. Kate blinked hard, as though expecting Neil to appear when she opened her eyes again. The wardrobe door was open, a coat hanger on the carpet in front of it. She crossed the room, energy suddenly bursting through her as she pulled open the doors to see what she already feared. His clothes were gone. She ran to her bedside table, dialling his number from the landline. It went straight to voicemail. *He must have it, he rang me from the side of the road. Did he ring on his phone, or use someone else's? Was his phone broken? Maybe it was lying on the floor of his mangled car?* She couldn't remember. She dialled the hospital and got put straight through to the operating theatres' office.

'It's Dr Harper. Is Neil back there now? With Jamie?'

'No, we haven't seen him. Jamie's still in surgery. He's doing okay. We'll have more of an update in a few hours. Get some rest, Doctor Harper.' Kate thanked the voice at the other end, not knowing or caring who it was.

She sat down on the bed, and looked around. Neil's laptop bag was gone, but she had no way of knowing what had been in the car. What the hell was going on?

* * *

Four Months Later

Kate watched as her radio alarm clock sprang to life, signalling the start of her day. She turned it off, not wanting to hear the happy chatty tones of the radio presenter as they celebrated another day dawning, waking the world up with their dull small talk about the weather, the traffic, the latest fashion faux pas of the rich and famous. She stretched lazily, her body not willing to leave the relative comfort of her single bed. She looked around her room, taking in the depressingly stark surroundings that she now called home. Her comfy king-sized bed at her house knocked spots off this one, but she hadn't spent a night there since the accident. She doubted that she ever would again. Going back for clothes was bad enough; the last time she had filled her car to the brim, carrying all she could, knowing that it would be a long while before she ever went there again, the 'for sale' sign outside reminding her of how much had changed since Iraq.

She went into the wardrobe, selecting a clean starched work uniform from the pile. She showered in the en suite, brushing her teeth, not bothering to even look in the mirror, let alone apply war paint to cover up her pale, drawn face. The bags under her eyes made her look haunted, a shadow of the person she once was. She brushed out her blonde hair, tying it tightly into a low ponytail, and putting on her shoes, she let the door lock behind her and headed for Trevor's office.

When he had followed her home after his tour was over, a month after she'd come home herself, Trevor had hounded her, constantly contacting her any way he could, offering her a job and accommodation on site in the rehabilitation centre he now ran. The tour had been his last, and he wanted to put down roots. He was being headhunted to run the state-of-the-art centre, nestled in Yorkshire. The first of its kind in the area, it would house several dozen war veterans, specialising in rehabilitation and prosthetics. The centre would also have an impressive program for PTSD sufferers, meaning that the wounded service personnel they took in had a one-stop shop at their fingertips, providing accommodation, a safe haven for their recovery and transition into life post-service. Trevor was so excited about the project that, eventually, Kate couldn't help but say yes. Her old job was no longer possible anyway, not now. And Trevor had made her an offer she couldn't refuse – so here she was.

'Morning, Trevor,' she said, sitting down in the chair opposite his large walnut desk. Trevor looked up from the pile of files he was poring over and winked at her, his grin dipping when he saw her.

'No sleep again? You need to get some rest you know, why don't you let me prescribe you something, to help you sleep?'

He didn't push it further. Kate had started shaking her head the minute the words had reached her ears. 'No. Thanks though. I need to be alert, in case.'

Trevor nodded, his lips pursing with the effort of keeping his thoughts to himself.

'We have a new intake today, and I want you to be his doctor.' He passed the file over to her, and got up, walking to the kettle which stood on the small kitchen area he had in his office. Kate looked at the label on the folder and pushed the file away with one finger.

'No, Trevor, you can't give him to me,' she said, turning around in her chair to face him, crossing her arms across her chest huffily. *He can't be here. Karma, stop messing with me, you evil bitch.* He ignored her, pouring a large cup full of hot water. He stirred in coffee and sugar, repeating the action in another cup. He added milk to both and handed one cup to her without even asking if she wanted it. She took it gratefully, gulping at the steaming hot drink as best she could without burning her lips. He sat back down at his desk, taking a swig – whilst pushing the file back over to her side of the desk.

'I can, and I will,' he said, forcefully. 'I'm aware of the possible ramifications, but I don't think it will be an issue. You know his case better than anyone, and his transition has not been... easy.'

'It won't work,' she said, pouting like a petulant teenager. 'He said I was lucky not to get sued last time I saw him.' *Second to last. A flash of a memory popped into her head. Chopper blades, panic. His voice in her head. Strong, commanding, his hand soothing. I'm here.* 'He could kick up a real shitstorm. You know that, right?'

Trevor smiled and waggled his eyebrows at her. She resisted the urge to stick her tongue out at him. She hated his bloody chirpy demeanour on a morning. She couldn't raise half of his optimism after a full night's sleep and a vat of coffee, and she didn't want to try.

'Trust me,' was all he said. 'He won't like it, but he won't sue.'

'Trust you?'

'Yes. Trust me. I think you can help him, Kate. God knows no one else has gotten through to him. I think you're the best person for the job. If he wants you off his case, I'll deal with it.'

'Fine,' she said tersely, reaching for the file. 'Your lawsuit.'

He grinned at his triumph. Kate wanted to poke his eyes out.

'How's your other patient today?' he asked, his tone softer.

Kate stood up, tucking the file under her arm and gripping the coffee cup in the other. 'Just the same.'

Trevor sat forward on his desk, resting his elbows on the table. 'You know what I'm going to say, Kate. You need to call Neil. You shouldn't be going through this on your own.'

'No,' Kate spat back harshly, splashing coffee down her arm. She let the hot liquid burn her skin and felt an odd sense of relief at the pain. *I am alive then*, she thought to herself. *Lovely.*

Trevor ignored her outburst, accustomed to her every mood after so much time working so closely together. He pushed a box of tissues across the desk, and she put the cup down, drying herself off. A splodge of brown coffee was spreading across the label on the file, and she dabbed at it ineffectually, only to see the stain spread across the name typed across the white surface. His name was tainted now, different, and there was no one to blame but herself.

'Is that all?' she asked, wishing the conversation away in her head. Trevor nodded, his face implying that he wanted to say more, but thankfully he kept silent and Kate left the room. Rounding the corner, she gripped the file tight to her chest, leaning against the wall for support. She could feel the blood pulsing in her ears, and her head swam. She closed her eyes and took deep breaths. *Pull it together, Kate, stop it. Get through the day, just get through the day.* She repeated her new mantra aloud, over and over, till the pulsing subsided and she trusted herself to move. She heard a noise and opened her eyes, looking down the corridor, hoping that no one saw the mad woman talking to herself and hugging the wall. No such luck. A nurse was walking down the corridor trundling a suitcase along with her, a man in a wheelchair just behind. He wasn't moving though, and her breath caught in her throat when she looked closer. The man had stopped his chair in the corridor, and was looking straight at her, a mixture of shock and disbelief in his features. Kate didn't linger on his tight lips or his furrowed brow though; she had been taken hostage by his eyes.

His big, green eyes, that were staring right back at her. One look into them, and she knew he had just witnessed her meltdown. She was grateful when the nurse addressed her. Nodding hello, she looked back at him, and he was still staring back at her. Looking away quickly, she turned on her heel and strode off down the corridor to her office.

* * *

Cooper

So, it was true. Someone up there really was having a laugh. I was dreading coming to this hippy hellhole as it was, but now I had the woman who sawed my leg off to look at every day. Just what every washed-up cripple needs. *What was she doing here? Had she known I was coming? From the look on her face, that was a no. He thought of her actions in the corridor. Her son. Maybe she's a mess, like me. Well, misery loves company.* I wheeled myself after the nurse, who was waddling down the corridor at a leisurely pace to my new room. Opening the double doors on the corridor, she pointed at a button on the wall. 'All the doors are opened by button entry, so no problem moving around the facility, and there is a call button in your room.'

I nodded once, glaring at the button as we passed through. Pressing a button like a child, whenever I needed help or simply wanted to open a door. It would be laughable if it wasn't so tragic. The nurse, a cheery looking rotund woman with 'Yvonne' sewn onto the lapel of her uniform glanced back at me, stopping outside a room labelled 'Room 15'. She pressed the button and walked through to the room, eyeing for me to follow. Once inside, she walked over to the curtains, opening them and cracking a window. Dust motes danced in the sunshine that fell onto the tiled floor and I squinted at the sudden change in light. 'You should have left them closed,' I growled, my short temper evident in my voice. It was ever present these days, having arrived on that chopper with me.

The nurse waved me away with her hand, choosing to ignore my obvious mood. 'No chance, you need some fresh air, a bit of sunlight. Makes all the difference to a day.'

I tutted, wheeling into the room slowly. It was clean enough, a carbon copy of the other rooms I had seen since getting here. Generic pictures on the cream-painted walls, thick, patterned curtains, minimal furniture. A wardrobe, chest of drawers, bedside table, and a custom hospital bed, complete with bed rails and soft mattress. I thought back to my last proper bed, before, back on the base – a ratty cot bed with scratchy blankets, the smell of the day's toil ground into the fabric. I would give anything right now to be back there, instead of in this glorified nursing home. Yvonne was starting to unzip my case now, and I shooed her away.

'Er, thanks, but I can unpack myself. Later.' She turned to look at me, opening her mouth as if to argue, but thought better of it and opened the door to the en suite. Another button.

'You have your bathroom here, pull cord on the wall if you need it. Anything else I can help you with?'

I shook my head, staring at my case, the wall, anywhere but in her direction.

Yvonne pursed her lips before smiling at me and turning to leave. I began closing the curtains, having already shut the low window. Then I heard her come back into the room, and she reached over my shoulder from behind me, dropping something in my lap – the induction pack.

'For you, when you're ready.'

I didn't turn around till the too-cheerful nurse had gone. I picked up the pack, breaking the seal. It was full of pamphlets and brochures on the centre, about the local help available, all the usual crap. It was then I spied a menu and a few other forms to fill in, and a schedule. Throwing the rest of the pack onto the bed, I looked at the daily plan the people in charge had made for me and froze when I spotted a familiar name. Kate Harper was on my schedule, every day for one-to-one rehabilitation. It had to be the same Kate as the one I just saw scraping herself off the corridor wall. I had made some enquiries after the time we spent together on the way home, but the hospital staff had been pretty tight-lipped about the whereabouts of the doctor and wouldn't answer any questions about her son or his wellbeing. Looking at her today though, it looked like she was struggling, so maybe her son really had died. Would she be back at work just a few short months later though? Had a tragedy like that happened to me, I would have used work to power through, so maybe that's just what she was doing.

I couldn't get a read on her; the woman who squeezed my hand as she slept, and urged me to live, that girl intrigued me and kept me up at night. The other half, the cold surgeon – this was the part I really couldn't get my head around. It looked like she had recognised me though, even though she didn't ac-knowledge it. I rubbed at my stump, trying to relieve the itching sensation I sometimes got. Moving to the bed, I looked in the pack for details of the gym. One thing that went in this place's favour was the workout facilities, and I could feel my muscles just dying for a good stretching. Exercise made me focus, distracted me from the thoughts and feelings that crashed into my brain, sending me crazy. Being stuck in this place was one thing, thinking about the next step was even worse – and I had no intention of taking that step anytime soon. Grabbing a towel from the top of the case, I pressed the button for the door to my new room and headed out to explore.

* * *

Kate was lying awake again, staring at the alarm clock, waiting for it to spring into action, spitting out the relentless cheerfulness that was morning radio. She reached for her phone and dialled a number, sighing deeply when the answering machine spoke out, informing her the mailbox was full and no message could be left. She threw her phone down on the mattress beside her, reaching over and slapping the alarm button hard when the clock struck the hour. Swinging her legs out of bed, she reached for her phone again, her hands shaking as she dialled. A ringtone echoed out into the quiet of the stark room, and Kate's breath held as it rang and rang. After an age, a croaky voice picked up, wearily saying 'hello' down the line.

Kate's heart was hammering in her chest as she heard the dulcet tones of her father-in-law.

'Roger, it's Kate. I am sorry to ring you so—'

'Kate? What's wrong?' His voice held concern, but she knew it was just him being polite. He didn't really care, he had already shown that much.

'Nothing is wrong, I'm just... I need to speak to Neil. Roger, we have to talk, and I can't get anywhere with his work, and his phone is off, and—'

'Kate,' Roger said, cutting her short. 'I don't fully understand what has gone on between you, but, after everything, I... he just doesn't want to be contacted by you, Kate, and I have to respect his wishes. You told him it was over, you can't have it how you want now.'

Kate gripped the phone tight, willing herself not to swear at the selfish prick of a man, defending his cowardly son. Years of being the quiet, dutiful partner, taking the scraps of 'kindness' her in-laws seldom threw, having to bite her tongue when they tried to tell her how to look after their son, while forsaking any interest in their own grandson. Every memory was a smouldering ember, floating around in the dark recesses of her memory, until now. Now, she let in the light, and the embers sparked against each other, fizzing and glowing into flames of fire. Between gritted teeth, she spoke slowly in a low, clear voice.

'When you play this conversation back in your head, years from now, I want you, both of you, to realise just how much of a mistake you made. Our marriage was over before I left for Iraq, but I'm not calling for me and you know it. This isn't about Neil, or me. The solicitors are dealing with all that. I want nothing from Neil, or you.' There was a surprised snort at the other end of the line, and Kate knew that her father-in-law was struggling to digest how she spoke to him. 'I will never contact you again, but if you have a heart, then you will ask your precious, spineless son, to call his ex-wife back. We have to sort this once and for all. You have my number.'

And she pressed the red button as forcefully as she could, suddenly wishing she had called on a landline so she could have slammed the receiver down, or even still had her mobile flip phone, so she could bang that shut. Pressing a button to end a call to a complete arsehole just didn't have the same satisfying effect, and she felt cheated. Cheated and impotent, just like she did every morning when she awoke, crying in the dark, alone.

8

COOPER

First morning of the touchy-feely bullshit rehab, and the good doctor was late. Only five minutes late, granted, but it still pissed me off. The army were big on time, so I was used to being organised with every minute of my day accounted for – not sitting here, watching the seconds and minutes of my life tick by. I'd been antsy all morning, wanting to see her. Not wanting to see her. Hell, I didn't know if I was mad at her, or just tormented by what I didn't know about her. I adjusted myself in the chair, trying to wake up my left bum cheek, which had fallen asleep. The lads in the gym had been great, and felt just like me – bored, missing the call of work, eager to pump some iron and feel the burn. They all had various degrees of injuries, but they didn't moan, and didn't ask questions, which was perfect for me. Denial is a wonderful thing, I find these days.

At Smithy's funeral, I had my first pity party, and I was in no hurry to go there again. Smithy's body was lying in a box, and people were milling around me, telling me how sorry they were for me, offering help, comfort. Why did I need that? Smithy was lost, and that was on me. My men made it home, sure, but what about the others? What about the fresh-faced souls heading out there now? There would be other kids on rooftops. Other soldiers not coming home. Would my absence be missed, or worse, would it have saved Smithy and others like him? I used to be sure of my position, steadfast in my abilities, but now I had nothing. Worst of all, I would never have a chance to do my bit again, to try to make up for the loss of my man by bringing others home in one piece.

The clock on the wall showed it was 9.10 a.m. Ten minutes late now. Ten minutes of rubbing my own arse cheek in this crap chair, waiting for someone to come and talk to me about how I should be coping. I was alive, so she'd already half won by leaving me that note. Brilliant. I took another sly look around the large room. On one back wall, laid out in racks, were legs of different sizes, colours, proportions. Fake legs to fit every stump. I looked away, subconsciously rubbing at the cut off sweat pant where my leg used to be. I didn't sleep well last night, kept awake by pain that made me want to scream, and this wasn't helping. I was just wheeling myself to the door to leave when it opened, and there she was.

She walked briskly into the room, thick black glasses perched on the end of her nose, her tousled blonde hair pinned up with pencils. The combination made her look like a sexy librarian. Or a sexy mad scientist, with the clipboard and white lab coat covering her body. I had a sudden curious thought. *What's under the coat, Doc?* I felt a twitch and looked away quickly. Twice this woman has done that to me. Last thing I needed was her rubbing up against me, making me grow a third leg. I cringed inwardly at my own daft joke. She stopped walking when she locked her eyes onto mine. Her expression was blank, and I matched it with one of my own, making sure to keep focused on her eyes, willing my erection to go. *You are maddening,* I wanted to tell her. I bit my lip to keep it in. We stared at each other, not moving, and I took the time to study her face, to suss out any clues about what had happened to the woman who saved my life against my wishes, for the last few months. She looked exhausted, the hollows under her blue eyes evident, even more so in the harsh strip lighting of the room. Her coat was pristine, clean and ironed, her black pumps looking like new, but the woman behind the mask was a wreck. She looked like a stiff breeze might blow her away.

'Damn, Missy,' I drawled. 'What happened to you?'

I was taking a chance on the nickname, chances were that she wouldn't recognise me, and probably had countless patients' faces in her head. As I waited for her response, I realised I didn't really know why I had the hope that she did. She blinked a few times and her shoulders seemed to drop a few inches. She smiled slightly, and walked over to me, bringing a chair with her.

'I told you, Captain, I don't care much for that nickname.'

I chuckled despite myself, partly from relief that she knew me, and partly due to her sarcastic retort. She looked different, but she still had a bit of fight left in her, underneath it all. I held my hands up, mocking surrender.

'So,' she said, flicking through the pages clipped to her board, keeping her eyes on the paper. 'I see you transferred from hospital, and you are here for rehabilitation and prosthetics. So far, apparently you have resisted all but the most basic care.'

I snorted, but she continued, the only sign she heard me being her slightly raised eyebrows. Oh, she was good at this. I felt the need to banter with her, see how much she would take before biting back, but something stopped me from letting rip just yet. I believed in what I fought for, and had I not been injured, I would still be out there with my buddies. I was angry, and this woman pushed all my buttons. I wanted to see the fire in her eyes flash, that grin of hers to show itself. Whenever I opened my mouth to say something cutting, I remembered her hand on mine when I woke up, broken and in pain. I remembered her face, full of gentle smiles and concern. I remembered her tears, and her words on that last day, and I wanted to figure out what happened, and just who Kate Harper was. She was here with Dr Tanner; I'd seen his name on the transfer forms. Looking across at her, I could tell she was pretending to study the clipboard, obviously waiting for me to speak. Her hands were curled tight around it, and I noticed that her fingers were ringless. I ran my fingers through my hair, which was far too long for my liking. I had to figure this woman out. She was messing with my head. I should hate her, but that faded a little the day in the chopper. It was hard to fuel it with her right here, in front of me.

'I'll do you a deal, Missy. You answer my questions,

and I'll try to get on with whatever you're trying to do with me here.' Her head jerked towards me, her eyes connecting with mine. She pushed up her glasses and lowered the clipboard.

'Even the leg?' she ventured.

I puffed air out through my cheeks, rubbing at the stubble on my chin. 'I'll see. The rest – yes. The leg? We can renegotiate.' I flashed her a cheeky grin. 'Depends on what goodies you give me.'

Kate flushed and put the clipboard back on the floor. The metal clip at the top made a clang on the sterile tiled floor. 'Then I reserve the right to not answer every single question.'

She had me there. 'Deal,' I said, holding out my hand. She went to stand but I stopped her by wheeling over to her. 'I'm a gent; I'll come to you.'

Our knees touched, and I put my hand forward, ignoring the sensation of heat that radiated from her into my right side. She touched my hand and shook it firmly. Why did it feel like a reward to touch her hand again?

'Thanks,' she said. 'I was just being polite, I'm not here to pander to you, so don't worry about that.'

I smiled at her. 'Do I look worried?'

Two hours later, and she was putting me through my paces. Upper arm workouts, measuring my body, making me stand out of the chair, working the bars. I kept looking at the prosthetics out of the corner of my eye. I didn't fancy going near those any time soon. Speaking to some of the guys at the gym, they seemed to have no problem with them, but the thought of the sores, the falls, the lack of dignity when your leg fell out from under you? No thanks. I'd be sticking to the chair for now. I was just glad that my arms could carry my weight still; I hadn't exactly been on my game of late. The last thing I wanted was to waste away to nothing.

She barked orders at me like a drill sergeant, writing copious notes on her little geek board, while I did my best to prove that I could do whatever she expected me to and more. By the end of the session, I was sweating profusely, and had a pain in my leg – the leg that wasn't there. It felt like my calf had cramped up, but I knew different. Funny thing, how the mind can play tricks. Bloody hilarious, in fact. I pushed myself to the end of the bars, reaching with one hand for my chair. I could feel Kate watching me from the corner of her eye, but she made no move to help, and I appreciated the fact that she was going to stick to her word. Sitting in the chair, I went to the towel rack, pulling one off and wiping myself down with it. My white tank top was stuck to me and my sweatpants were looking a little worse for wear too. Kate came over, bottle of water in hand. I eyed her but decided it wasn't babying me to bring me a drink, so I took it with a word of thanks and took a huge swig. She opened a bottle herself, taking a slow drink. I watched her delicate neck stretch up as she put the bottle to her lips. She was at least ten shades paler then when I saw her in Iraq, as though she had never seen a day of sunshine from then till now. Her skin was smooth, blemish free, with tendrils of knotted blonde hair around the nape of her neck and ear lobes. She looked exhausted, as though she had just rolled right out of bed into her clothes.

'So, this is it then? Five days a week you put me through my paces?'

She nodded, replacing the cap onto her bottle. She surprised me by kneeling at my foot. 'I... er,' she started cautiously. 'I need to check your wound site, if I may.'

I shook my head. 'Nope, not today, Missy. We'll leave that for another day, I think.'

She opened her mouth to protest, and I whipped out my hand without even thinking first, placing my index finger across her lips, shushing her. She didn't recoil as I thought she would, but instead she sucked in a quick breath, and we both looked at each other in shock. I slowly pulled my finger down her face, pulling my hand away from those soft and sassy lips. She licked at them, only stopping when a voice disturbed us from the doorway.

'Good first session?' Trevor asked, a strange expression on his face as he looked across at us. *Jealousy?* It didn't look that way, and I knew if Kate were mine, I would be more than pissed that a man had his hands anywhere near her. Not that it was like that, hell, I didn't even know what I was doing in my own mind. Kate sprang up from her position on the floor, dashing across the room, grabbing the clipboard on her way out. Passing Trevor, she lowered her eyes.

'Er, yes, not bad,' Kate mumbled, her face now a fetching shade of scarlet. An improvement to her usual alabaster, I couldn't help thinking. I tried not to smile as I imagined me being the reason for her sudden colouring. She pushed past Trevor awkwardly in the doorway, too awkwardly for two people that were intimate with each other. Maybe I was wrong. I squashed down the sudden surge of relief that I felt, squashed it deep in the dark. Perhaps I would bring that into the light later, when I could deal with it properly. A lot of thoughts lived in the dark corners of my mind these days, so it would have good company. Trevor watched Kate walk down the corridor, her shoes click-clacking on the floor as she strode away. He smiled at me then, coming into the room and taking residence in the chair that Kate had just vacated.

'So, Captain, you're finally here.' He grinned, and I smiled back.

'Don't be so modest – you put up a fair bit of a fuss to drag my ass here, didn't you?'

Trevor nodded contritely, unconcerned about being caught out. 'I heard you weren't doing well,' he said, not looking at me. 'This place is the answer.'

'I was doing just fine. So what's the plan?'

'The plan?' Trevor asked, picking a piece of lint off his brown slacks.

'Her,' I growled at him. 'Why have her as my therapist? She's a surgeon isn't she?'

'Yes, and a damn fine one.' Trevor looked straight at me, and I could see his jaw flexing under his skin. He was hiding something, I knew it.

'It just strikes me as weird, to put me with her. I threatened to sue her, and you assign me to her roster? Why is she even doing this job? How does a surgeon go from doing that to this?'

Trevor rubbed his hand down the length of his jaw, tapping his fingers on his chin. 'I needed to fill a job, Kate took it.'

'That's it?' I asked, annoyed by his evasive answer.

'Yep. She's more than qualified,' he replied. 'She started out in physio before becoming a surgeon.'

'That doesn't answer my question.'

'I've worked with her on and off for years,' he added. 'There's nothing more to it.' *Fine, play it that way.* 'I just ask,' he continued, 'that you give her a shot. She can help you, but you have to cut her some slack, give her a chance.'

I looked down at my legs in the chair instinctively. Whenever I thought of Kate in a favourable way, whenever I thought of the way she held my hand, or talked to me in that soft whispering voice, I took one look at my leg and reminded myself that she was the reason I was still here, on this planet, like this. I would have preferred to just go out, just let the injuries and the pain take me away. End of. Nice army burial, with my comrades. Not this. I had turned from a happy, committed guy to a bitter old man, all in the space of a few months. Pity party for one, anybody? Who wants to see that? I was a lost cause, sentenced to this chair and a life of regrets and loneliness. The thing was, whenever I looked at Kate, I saw my own fears mirrored in her face, in her haunted, tired eyes, and that stirred something in me. It reminded me of her words that day, telling me to fight, and the pain on her face when she talked about her son. And now she was here, and Trevor was giving me mixed messages. *Why put us together if he was worried about protecting her?*

I folded my arms, resting my elbows on my chair. I realised Trevor was waiting for me to speak, but I wouldn't give him the satisfaction of acting like I was interested. I didn't know how to play this yet, but that was my business. Kate intrigued me, and the truth was that I wanted to see her again. I couldn't put my finger on the reason why just yet. Trevor cracked.

'Look, I know you're having issues dealing with the changes in your life since the explosion. Anyone would struggle, but you have to let someone in to help you. I really believe that Kate could be the one to do that. She is the only one I have ever seen you take any notice of, and despite your short and complicated history, I think this will work. I just ask that you bear in mind, she has her own scars to bear. Don't be a complete jerk.'

I laughed out loud before I could even think about being mad. Trevor looked surprised and bemused at my outburst, which made me laugh even more. I went for the door, still laughing as I went. As I pressed the button for the door, I turned back to him.

'Trevor, I will be a perfect gent. I promise.'

I could hear Trevor's disbelieving chuckle in reply

as I headed to my room. For the rest of the night, I thought about those scars. I needed to know the answers, and if I kicked her off my physio, I wasn't going to get them. Trevor knew what he was doing, I'd give him that. Missy was under my skin, whether I liked it or not. I'd play the game for now. It wasn't like I had anything else to do with my time. After a shower, a change of clothes and some food, I went to bed, flicking the buttons on the remote to try and find something to watch. I needed to see if this place had a library. The battered paperback I brought with me had long been read, and I was beyond bored with the incessant drone of the television. After the fourth celebrity advert promoting their latest workout DVD, I turned off the TV, giving up. I reached for the overbed tray and picked up the tatty book. Nestled amongst the pages was a well-thumbed piece of paper. Self-consciously flicking my eyes to the closed front door, I opened the paper gently. Kate's words, now imprinted in my brain, danced across the page in her hurried scrawl. I had looked at this paper so many times now that I could probably recite it word for word, and it always gave me comfort when I did. *Maybe you want her here, Coop.* I ran my thumb along the grooves on the paper, where she had pressed pen to paper hard to sign her name. I refolded the letter and tucked it back into its hiding place. Staring up at the ceiling, I tried to think of something else, but my mind soon wandered back to thoughts of Kate, and her son. *Well, Coop, you heard him. Time to stop being a complete jerk. Or try at least.*

9

Kate flew through her paperwork that evening, and eventually collapsed into a heap after her usual nightly routine. The day after her first session with Captain Cooper, she was up, showered and dressed before her alarm clicked into life, and she switched it off on her way out of the door, key card and clipboard in place.

She was on her way to her 9 a.m. appointment with Cooper before she realised that she hadn't yet eaten. Running her hand over her tight bun, she could feel the dryness of her hair, and she sighed dramatically as she walked down the long corridor. Time stood still here; it was a world away from the fast-paced terror and adrenaline of the warzone, and Kate missed that every single day. Here, everything seemed so much slower, bleaker. It was like living in a sterile bubble, away from the real world and all of its colour. The longer she was there, the less like herself she felt. She wore a mask all day long, and the only sanctuary she had was in her room at night, where she was alone. The trouble was, that was the time she dreaded the most, and she couldn't see a way out, a way through this limbo of isolation and heartbreak. How life changed quickly, she thought to herself. She thought she had problems a few months ago... She would gladly go back and deal with all that now with a song in her heart, rather than the reality of today. Dry hair and her aching husk of a body were the least of her problems.

She was just walking into the therapy suite when Zach, one of the porters, came out. They almost knocked into each other, Zach swerving at the last minute. He was chuckling to himself as he looked at her. 'Have a good morning, Doc,' he said, a cheesy grin on his face. Kate watched him walk away, wondering what had tickled him. She opened the door and was greeted by a strange sight. Cooper was sitting at one of the tables, tucking into a bacon sandwich. The smell in the room made her mouth water, and she licked her lips before she could stop herself.

He turned to look at her when the door squeaked her arrival, and he flashed her a grin, or as best a grin he could muster with a mouthful of bacon. He swallowed quickly, motioning her to come in. He pulled out the chair nearest to his wheels and patted the seat.

'Come on in, Missy. I wasn't sure what you'd like, so I got some fruit too in case you're a vegetarian or something.' He said 'vegetarian' like some people would say 'traffic warden' or 'herpes'. She stood stock still in the doorway, and he kept his sparkling green eyes on her, raising an eyebrow when she didn't answer. 'You going to move, or what?' He waggled his eyebrows then, producing a tall cup of shop-bought coffee. 'Caramel latte?'

Kate smiled then, despite herself. The man had got her favourite coffee. Damn him. She walked over to the table, setting her things to one side, and took the large cup gratefully. She took a sip and sighed, relief flowing through her as her body accepted the sweet shot of caffeine. Her eyes closed as she savoured the feeling. When she opened them again, he was looking at her, a look of amusement mixed with something else, something she couldn't quite work out.

'Better?' he asked, his voice gravelly. He licked a dab of tomato sauce from his thumb, and Kate found she had to look away. She could feel her face flushing.

'Much,' she nodded. 'But how did you...'

Cooper tapped the side of his nose. 'I have my contacts. No way was I going to drink the swill in those machines.'

Kate laughed. Just once, but it was there. It hung in the air between them, a rare sound, and then it was gone. Cooper passed across a brown package, and a sachet each of tomato and brown sauce. 'Bacon sandwich?'

She reached for the tomato sauce, ripping open the brown paper. 'Yes please, but brown sauce belongs with sausage sandwiches only.' Cooper gave her a sideways glance, a funny expression on his face.

'What?' she said, taking the first bite of the delicious hot breakfast. She had to stop herself from moaning with pleasure at the taste, after living on the 'healthy' food they provided in the centre.

'Nothing,' he said, an amused grin betraying his poker face. They sat and ate in companionable silence, and Kate was so hungry and grateful for the food that she found her mood had much improved.

'So,' Cooper said. 'Do you like it here?'

Kate swallowed her mouthful, considering her answer. *No, I hate every second of every day, of my entire life.* Not the way to go. *Yes, because I don't have to face the world.* No, not that either.

'It's okay,' she settled for saying.

'Only okay?' he pressed gently. Kate kept her eyes on her breakfast.

'It's a job, Captain. Trevor needed the help, so I came.'

Coop finished the dregs of his coffee. 'Fair enough. Shall we get started then? Don't want Trevor to think we're slacking in here, eh?' He started to pick up the debris from the table, resting it on his knees, then deposited the lot in the bin. Kate didn't move to help; she knew he would hate it and she didn't want to disturb his seemingly cheerful mood. Whatever made this day easier would be welcome. Finishing the last of her coffee, she stood and followed him to the bin, dumping her rubbish next to his. Wiping her hands, she reached for the clipboard. 'Let's get to work.'

A few hours later, and it was time for lunch. The facility used a cafeteria style of dining, with vending machines for out of hours snacking. Kate had access to a kitchen area but had yet to even think about travelling to the nearest supermarket to stock up. This morning's breakfast treat had reminded her of just how much she missed decent coffee though, and she figured she had to at least consider the trek, perhaps the next day off she got.

Rita gave her a smile as she took her place in the

lunch queue. 'Afternoon, Dr Harper, how are we doing on this fine day?'

Kate smiled at her, taking a tray from the stack. 'Rita, please, just call me Kate.'

Rita winked. 'No point you doing all those years in school for me to call you Kate, is there? I like Doctor Harper anyway, sounds sophisticated.'

Kate shook her head good-naturedly. 'What's good today then?'

'Rita, if I didn't know better, I would say that the good doctor here was dissin' your food.' Kate whirled around, and almost clonked Cooper on the head with her tray.

'Hey,' he said, putting his hands up in mock defence. 'Come on then, put 'em up, show me what you got, Missy!'

Kate put the tray back onto the service area, face bright red.

'Captain, I'm sorry, you—'

'Ooh, Captain, is it?' Rita chuckled. 'You people with your titles, so funny!'

Cooper lowered his fists then, taking a tray from the stack himself. 'You have a good point there, Rita. Tell you what, Doc, since we had our first breakfast together this morning, you can call me Thomas. Or Cooper, whichever. You have seen me naked, remember?' He threw Kate a positively devilish look, and Rita guffawed.

'Well, it's all coming out now!' She cackled as she walked into the kitchen area out back.

'Thanks for that,' Kate groaned. Kate selected a tray of salad and some warm chicken breasts, noticing that Cooper was laughing to himself beside her. He selected a plate with a beef burger and chips on, grabbing a side salad and an orange juice and laying them out on his tray. Ignoring him, Kate went for a bottle of water and turned to the nearest empty table to sit. Trevor often joined her, but today he was busy with meetings, so she was solo. She was just contemplating the rest of her day when the chair next to hers was abruptly yanked aside. Cooper put his tray down on the table, settling his chair into place.

'Do you mind?' she asked, mouth agape.

Cooper frowned. 'Mind what, what have you done?' He cut his burger in half, before popping a warm chip into his mouth.

'I haven't done anything, but you just told Rita I've seen you naked!'

'I know,' he chuckled. 'Good times.' Cooper ripped into the burger, turning to give Rita a thumbs up. She was setting more food out, and blew him a kiss in response, which made her kitchen assistant, Tyler, laugh out loud and roll his eyes. Kate willed the flush in her face to settle as she cut through her chicken breast.

'You really are a surgeon, aren't you?' Cooper asked, looking at the way she had cut her chicken into neat, even portions.

Kate ignored him, tossing the chicken pieces into her salad with a fork, and adding dressing. 'That your first question, or was that the vegetarian enquiry earlier?'

Cooper shook his head, finishing his mouthful. 'Oh no, those questions will be coming, don't you worry. I thought we could start this afternoon. You prepared, Missy?'

Kate ignored the annoying nickname he'd bestowed on her. Looking into his bright green eyes with all the game face she could muster, she wrinkled her nose. 'Bring it, Cooper.'

She took a mouthful of salad, but it stuck in her throat. An orderly was wheeling a patient into the dining area. Sitting them at a small table in the corner of the room, setting the brake on the chair before talking into his patient's ear then joining the lunch queue.

'Why is he in here?' she said quietly, almost to herself.

'Why is who in here?' Cooper asked, following her gaze.

Kate didn't answer, she was already up on her feet. She approached the chair, which contained a very sad looking little boy. Pale-faced, gaunt even. He was wearing the latest trainers and a pair of tracksuit bottoms similar to the ones that Cooper himself wore. The darkness of the green on the youth's Minecraft T-shirt gave the boy's skin an eerie translucent quality, the opposite to how healthy a child looked when a buttercup was held under their chin. Kate lowered herself to her knees next to his chair, taking his hand, but the boy moved his away, twisting his head to look out of the window, above her head. Kate looked like she was going to speak, but she just patted one of the boy's knees, and standing up, she headed out of the doors, not looking at anyone or stopping to pick up her lunch. Cooper looked at the boy, who hadn't moved but was still looking out of the window. Kate's untouched lunch, lettuce still stuck in the fork prongs, sat on the tray in front of him. Rita appeared at his side then, and she packaged the lunch back into its plastic container.

'You're working with Dr Harper this afternoon, right? Will you take her lunch please? That girl needs to eat, though lord knows what salad and water will do.'

Cooper nodded, finishing his meal quickly as his gaze darted to the boy. As Rita passed by his table again, Cooper reached for her arm.

'What's the deal there, anyway?'

Rita looked from him to the boy, and back again, a conflicted look on her face. One thing Rita wasn't, was a gossip, but as she looked at Cooper again, she seemed to make an agreement with her own conscience, and she sat down in Kate's seat.

'That's her boy, right there.' Cooper's head snapped back to the lad, a boy he had thought long dead. Now as he looked at the lad's stubborn profile, jaw flexing, he could see it. See Kate in him, from the bow of his lips to the curve in his nose. 'There was an accident, when she was serving overseas. The poor mite will never walk again, and he hates the world and his mother for it.'

So that was why she was here. It made some sense now, why a talented woman like her would want to be here. She was here to help her son. Cooper finished his food. He squeezed Rita's hand once, and she gave him a sad smile.

'Rita, you still got some of that chocolate cake left?'

Rita gave him an 'atta boy' wink and scuttled off to the kitchen.

Cooper set the slice of cake on the table. The ceramic clinked on the Formica surface. He stuck a fork into the top of the moist, gooey piece of heaven.

'Hi,' he tried.

The boy didn't even flinch, he just kept looking out of the window. Following his gaze, he saw two of the guys from the gym playing hoops outside, taking it in turns to throw the basketball into the net.

'Hello?' Cooper ventured, careful to keep the deepness of his voice to a low rumble. Nothing. The men outside continued to play, their shoulders and upper arms glinting in the sunlight, showing their exertion. Cooper watched them awhile too, their easy play seemingly taunting the two people staring from behind the glass. Observers of life in all its simplistic glory. Cooper looked to his right and saw that the boy was now observing him from the corner of his eye, looking him up and down.

'The leg, right?' he asked. The boy's eyes snapped to his, his face still showing no emotion. *He has her eyes,* he thought with a jolt. It was like looking at Kate, blue eyes full of suspicion, fear, sorrow. He found himself wishing he could take all that away, for them both.

He tapped his thigh. 'It's okay, it doesn't hurt.' *Not*

much now, anyway. Apart from the nights I wake up bathed in sweat, agony pulsing from the leg that isn't there any longer.

He pushed the plate a little closer. 'That's for you. I have to go now, Dr Harper is helping me get better.' The boy stiffened at the sound of his mother's name, and Cooper's brow furrowed. *What was the deal with those two?* 'I'll leave that with you. It's pretty good.'

Cooper went to leave the dining room, calling at the kitchen door on his way out. Rita was scrubbing down the surfaces, and she smiled when she saw him.

'Any joy?' she asked kindly, bringing him two neatly wrapped Tupperware containers. He took them with a nod of thanks.

'Nope, not really – unless you count eye contact.'

Rita looked at the boy and raised her eyebrows. 'Well, I've been trying to fatten that boy up for weeks, but it's not me who got him to eat the cake now, is it?'

Sure enough, when Cooper glanced across, there he was. Eating cake. Rita squeezed his shoulder.

'I know that Kate is supposed to help you, but I see it a little differently.' She came round to his side and dipped to plant a kiss on his stubbly cheek. He rolled his eyes, but was touched by the gesture. 'I think that you can all do a lot to help each other.'

She patted the boxes sat on his lap. 'Now get gone

with you, I have cooking to do, and you have a hungry woman waiting for you.'

He flashed her a look, shocked at her choice of words. She swatted at him with a tea towel hanging from her waist. 'Oh, come on, don't be a shrinking violet. You're not dead yet you know.'

Cooper thought about her words all the way to the rehab room. *Not dead yet.*

* * *

Kate looked up at the ticking clock. Cooper was late, and she didn't even have the energy to care, let alone hunt him down and drag him to therapy. She looked at the file in front of her. She didn't even have any work to do. In her old job, there would always be lots to do, even after the last patient had been stitched up. Paperwork used to drive her crazy, but now she would be glad of it, would welcome it even. Having one patient was unfamiliar territory, and having one patient as stubborn as Captain Cooper, with their complicated history, was alien. Jamie flashed into her mind, and she physically winced at the memory. *What on earth was she going to do? She knew she couldn't carry on like this, but there was no way out. Every day was the same.*

Till now. Now, she had the comments and penetrating stares of her patient to deal with.

The squeak of the door heralded the arrival of someone in the room. A masculine hand came into her point of view, pushing two plastic containers onto the table in front of her.

'I got Rita to bag your lunch, and I snagged some of her excellent cake too.'

Kate smiled thinly, taking the lid off the salad. She tucked in, using the cutlery wrapped in a napkin that Cooper held out to her.

'Thanks, I was pretty hungry. I don't want the cake though.' She pushed the container aside, back towards him. He shrugged, and taking off the lid, he stuck a spoon into the soft top layer of the dark slab. 'No worries, I'll just leave it here. I'll make a start while you eat, just in case the Trevornator shows his face.' He went over to the weights, picking some up and getting to work. Ten minutes later, he chanced a sly glance across at the good doctor and found she was taking a spoonful of the dessert. Smiling to himself, he carried on working. *Like mother, like son.*

10

FOUR MONTHS EARLIER

Kate slammed through the doors of A & E, still clad in her army fatigues. She knew she looked a mess but she didn't care. She felt disgusting, dirty, but as soon as they had landed she had begged a lift from a passing officer and raced to her boy. She could feel the layer of dirt and dust that permeated her clothes, and she felt at odds with the bright white sterile starkness of the hospital reception. One of the receptionists recognised her, dashing around the desk.

'Dr Harper, come with me.' She nodded and followed dumbly, vaguely aware of the looks of sympathy the other staff behind the desk shot her when they heard her name. She dared not look at them, for fear their expressions would confirm the worst. Confirm without a doubt what she had feared since getting that call, that Jamie was dead. Her phone was in her kit bag, but like her, it was having trouble adjusting to the last few hours, and she couldn't get a signal. She had received no news since the call from Neil, and it was freaking her out. She became aware that the receptionist was talking to her, holding and stroking her hand as they walked briskly from white corridor to white corridor. She couldn't seem to make herself tune in, to hear the words the woman was churning out. She only saw one thing. SPINAL UNIT. The words, in huge white letters on the wall, jolted her into the present.

'He's not dead?' she asked, confused. The receptionist stopped then, taking Kate's face between her own two soft hands. 'No! No, Doctor Harper, your son is alive.'

'But... why?' she asked, her words cutting out like failed fireworks. 'Why?' she tried again, forcing the very word from her chest.

The receptionist steered her to a chair, patting her hand and scuttling off.

Kate sat there, staring at the empty corridor, for a decade. It had to be a decade, it could be no less. Every second signified a week, every minute even longer. She felt as though her whole life experience was on this hard plastic chair, sitting in this corridor, her eyes smarting from the starkness of the white surroundings.

She thought of the day that Jamie had come into the world. Expecting her son to be late, as first babies and boys often were, she was at work, squeezing every second out of her maternity leave. Or so she told people. The truth was, the thought of being at home with a newborn with no work to challenge her was terrifying. There, in the hospital, she knew what to do. Broken bones, poking through skin and sinew, she loved. Mending people, fixing their injuries, helping them to walk, to hold their loved ones, to work – that gave her a high that she felt sure no infant would. Even hers.

So, when her waters broke two weeks early, just as she had finished setting a dislocated shoulder, no one was more surprised than her. She wanted to shout out, 'No, it's too early, come back in a fortnight', but of course, baby waits for no nervous mother. Neil was away at a conference, the nurses frantically trying him all day. Nine hours later, exhausted, sweaty and angry at Neil for being sat in some hotel listening to some bore with a flipchart instead of with her, Kate gave one final push and felt her son slide from her body. He was placed on her tummy, Kate reaching for him instinctively, a mewling, purple sticky mess. She cut the cord herself, ending their journey as it had begun, just the two of them, and she waited for the nurses to check him over. She sat and chomped and slurped at her tea and toast, suddenly ravenously hungry and thirsty. She had always wondered at such a strange tradition, giving a new mother builder's tea and white toasted bread slathered in butter – such an English thing to do after squeezing a small person from your own hoo-ha, but it was the best thing she had ever tasted.

Her son snuffled as they checked him over, giving one lusty cry as they prodded and poked at him, and then he was there. All wrapped in borrowed clothes, with her own overnight bag at home, not yet packed. He looked out at the world from his blanket peephole, a lone curl of dark hair licking the brim of his tiny blue hat. Kate held him in her arms, and the world she knew ended. One look into those blue eyes, and she knew, no matter where her work took her, it would be the two of them, together, forever. As she spoke to her son silently in her head, he reached out a wrinkled hand, touching her face, and she knew he understood. Her Jamie.

* * *

Dr Stuart Jenkins, the hotshot spinal surgeon at the hospital Kate worked at, was arrogant but respected. Kate herself had often crossed paths with him professionally, their skills often being required simultaneously, and she had a grudging respect for him and his practices. The nurses hated him, but he got the job done.

He stood in front of her now, still in scrubs, a smattering of blood on his clothing. Kate couldn't bring herself to look at him, and chose to focus on the blood. Her son's blood, no doubt. His lifeforce, there on her colleague's uniform, like paint flecks on a contractor. He moved then, kneeling before her. His hand on her knee, warm and clean. She wondered where those hands had just been, working on her son's body.

'Kate,' he murmured softly. 'Kate, we have to talk.'

She looked at him then, his deep brown eyes soft and warm. He spoke in terms she understood, no layman's speak; he told her straight, gave her the facts. All Kate could grasp was the fact that he said spinal compression. When he spoke of permanent lower paralysis, and wheelchairs, Kate stopped listening. All she could think about was the promise she had made her newborn son, the promise of the two of them, together forever.

From that day to this, Kate had never been far

from Jamie's side, but the Jamie she knew was gone. The boy she saw that day, tubes everywhere, sleeping off the cocktail of drugs in the large white bed, his thick dark lashes fluttering against the white pillowcase, was not her Jamie. This boy was broken, fractured, beaten. His face, swollen from the impact, cut from the glass shards, was unrecognisable from the cheeky boy she had left, and she hated Neil for it. She hated him for not protecting their boy, not shielding him from danger, but he wasn't the one she hated the most. It wasn't the driver of the other car either, a woman on her way to the gym after the school run, now utterly ruined by that morning. It wasn't her fault. Neil had been the one distracted, pulling into her lane, putting her life at risk as well as his own – and his only child's. She didn't hate them, she saved that venomous hate for somewhere far closer to home. For herself.

11

Kate stared at her alarm clock, watching the seconds tick by to her alarm time. Again. Tick, tick, tick. Rolling onto her back, she lifted up her T-shirt and looked at the hollows near her hips, above her knickers. She had lost more weight. She could feel her ribs as she rested her arms along the side of her body. During her first years as a doctor, she had grown thin and gaunt – a mixture of long hours, no sleep and no food – and her colleagues at the time had been so worried. She wondered what they would make of her now, thinner still. Her hair felt lank as she pinned it back. Trevor knew better these days than to mention anything to her, choosing instead to look at her meaningfully when she saw him, communicating with his eyes his unspoken concern for her. She thought of Cooper then, feeding her cake and thick calorie-laden coffees. She had to admit, the thought of a nice caramel latte this morning made her want to leave her room for once. Turning off the alarm as it whirred into life, she dressed and went to leave the room, stopping herself at the door when she caught sight of herself in the mirror.

Turning back to her dressing table, after a good rummage in her drawers, she slicked on some light lipstick, a little touch of blusher onto her cheeks and a spritz of her favourite perfume. Looking back into the mirror, she saw a glimpse of her old self staring back, and almost smiled.

Leaving her room, she headed straight for her regular 8 a.m. meeting. Opening the door, she started to say 'good morning' when a plastic cup sailed past her head. Ducking at the last minute, she watched as the water shimmered in the morning sunlight as it cascaded down the wall. The beaker settled at her feet. Bending down to scoop it up, she placed it on the nearby dresser. One of the regular nurses, Fran, was pleading with Jamie, trying to get him to put a jumper over his head. Kate stepped into the room and tried to help, but Jamie was flailing around, batting them both away. Kate looked across at Fran, and noticed she was bleeding from a small cut on her forehead.

'Fran!' Kate exclaimed. 'What the hell happened?' Fran, giving up on putting Jamie's jumper on, sighed and sat at the edge of the bed.

'I'm okay, it was the photo frame. I didn't duck in time,' she quipped, but Kate could tell by her face she was in pain. She spied the photo frame by her feet, a picture of her in the hospital, holding an hour-old Jamie. The glass was smashed into shards around her feet, and the wooden frame was hanging off on two corners.

'Fran, you go and get that checked out, I will deal with all this.'

Fran frowned at her, not moving. 'You sure?' she asked, sounding uncertain. Jamie had taken off the jumper and was scowling at them both in the corner.

'Yeah, I'm sure,' she replied, smiling at Fran fondly. 'Thanks, hun, and sorry. I'll deal with this.'

Jamie snorted from his chair, and Kate marvelled at the normal youthful sound he had produced for once. Fran wiped at the blood that was dripping down her face then left.

'What the hell are you playing at, Jamie? Huh?' Kate cried, grabbing the wastepaper basket and getting carefully to her knees. She started to pick up the glass, moving the frame to the side. It was utterly broken, but thankfully the photo was still intact. She tucked it into the pocket of her long cardigan, a staple wardrobe accessory for her uniform these days, with her feeling so cold all the time. No reply came, and Kate continued to clear the floor till she was sure all the glass had been cleaned up. She went to pick up the jumper, folding it up and putting it back into the drawer. Jamie only had a flimsy T-shirt on, and she knew that he would be taken out today, around the grounds of the centre. Pulling out another hoodie, she showed it to her son. 'This one?'

The icy stare he gave her told her that this garment wasn't favoured either. She pulled a face at him, gurning her lips and sticking her tongue out, and for a fraction of a glorious second, she saw a glimpse of a smile from her son, but it was soon gone. Her heart leapt at the thought, and she felt the pain of its loss once more. Where had her son gone? The boy she had left behind for a warzone had gone, disappeared, and in his place was this sullen, broken, angry young man. *How did it go? Time to put away childish things? Well, the childish thing was her son, and she wasn't quite ready to put him away yet.* Every morning she tried to get through to him. Saw Cooper in him. The anger and rage at having his life as he knew it stolen from him. Jamie had been so active, so happy with his friends. Playing sports. Riding his bike. Going to school. Everything, like Cooper, had changed. Been taken away from him. And like Cooper, he blamed her. Was angry at her. She couldn't bear it. Didn't know how to get through to him. All of her training went out of the window when it came to her son. So they were here, trapped together in this new nightmare.

Sighing loudly, she passed him the hoodie. He took it from her, and she was just enjoying her little triumph when it came whizzing past her head. She said nothing, picking it back up and passing it to him again. This happened non-stop for the next five minutes, her passing him the sweatshirt, him throwing it back at her like a toddler playing a game in a high chair. On what felt like the fiftieth throw, Kate snapped. 'Jamie, put the damn thing on! It's cold outside, you need it on!'

He glared at her, turning his chair to the window. Kate felt so angry she had to clench her fists and take a breath to stop herself strangling her son where he sat. She brushed away hot tears, blinking furiously. 'Fine,' she said to the back of his head, when she trusted her voice not to break. She stormed out of his room and didn't look back. Once again, she'd done the wrong thing, and made everything worse. She headed to her next appointment. *Time to screw up another life.*

* * *

Cooper had dragged himself out of bed this morning, after a night of sweats, pain and terror. He had resisted the urge to strip the sheets before the cleaners came in, for fear that they would think he had wet the bed, rather than saturated it with sweat. He had enough indignities in his life, without people thinking that he had peed himself too. Around 5 a.m. he had resorted to lying on the bathroom floor, where at least he could feel the coolness of the tiles against his hot skin. The pains shooting down his leg had eventually abated around dawn, and he had slept a little, sat bolt upright against the sink pedestal. When he awoke at half past seven, he was so grateful that he wasn't in pain he nearly wept. It was happening more often now, something he thought he might have escaped post-amputation. Cooper wasn't afraid of much in life, but those pains did terrify him. The pain ran from the top of his hip to the tips of his non-existent toes, and he didn't want to start taking painkillers. He didn't want to become dependent like so many of his comrades had, so he kept quiet. *What kind of man mouned about pains in his leg, when his leg wasn't even there?* He swore he could feel the pains, shooting down his nerves, muscles – all things no longer a part of him. His stump felt sore today, but he wasn't sure whether that was in his head, or because he had given it a few good thumps in the night, trying to shock his body out of itself. It didn't work.

By 8.30 a.m., Captain Thomas Cooper was dressed in his workout gear, sat in his chair, heading to therapy via his usual morning coffee pick-up. The only signs that he was anything less than composed were his stubble, now longer than usual, his red eyes, and his expression. If you looked at him fast enough, you could still see the slight look of fear in his eyes, before it turned back to stony arrogance.

Kate was raring to go as she walked into the treatment room that morning; ready to put Cooper through his paces, to take her mind off Jamie and the sheer frustration she felt. She bounced into the room, clipboard held tightly under one arm, and an air of determination firmly set on her features. Cooper was sat at the table, a bacon sandwich between his meaty hands. He looked at her, one eyebrow raised in a question. She faltered in her step, catching herself quickly. Putting the clipboard to one side, she crossed her arms.

'Ready for a busy morning, Captain? We have lots to do today, and I have decided that today is the day when we look at that leg.' She fixed him with a stare, hoping he wouldn't see her nervousness underneath. He frowned slightly, wiping at his mouth with a napkin, before silently pushing a large paper cup of coffee towards her. She shook her head, ignoring the pull of caffeine he had dangled in front of her. 'No thanks, I'd rather get cracking.'

He shrugged and pushed the cup closer still with his fingertips. She noticed his hand shook a little with the small gesture and looked closer at him. He looked tired, less put together than usual. She was just wondering what was wrong when he spoke.

'Drink your coffee, Missy. It's getting cold, and I still have my breakfast to have. We won't be doing any therapy today. I declare today "skivers day".'

She looked at him, incredulous. 'Skivers day? Are you for real? I *work* here you know, supposedly helping you, and you want a day off? I don't think so.'

Cooper looked across at her, and she noticed the red lines around his eyes, which were bloodshot. 'Well Missy, you'd better go and find someone else to work on then, because I'm doing nothing today.'

He dismissed her with his eyes then, returning to his breakfast in silence. Kate didn't know whether to punch him or cry. *Was it pick-on-Kate day today?* She could feel the tears welling up, and a hard lump forming in the back of her throat. *Fine,* she thought to herself. She started to walk to the table, but instead of taking the coffee, she kept walking until she was behind Cooper. He turned in surprise, but she was too fast. Taking the brake off the chair, she wheeled him towards the door. He still had his coffee in one hand and a bacon sandwich in the other, so he couldn't do much to stop her. He started to put his leg down on the floor, but she tilted the chair back, causing a drip of coffee to fall onto his crotch. 'Hey!' he said, stopping the struggle. He looked back at her, a mixture of surprise and anger on his face. 'What the hell are you doing? Stop this damn chair, NOW!' he bellowed. Kate kept wheeling, shouting 'No!' into his face. His eyebrows shot up in shock, and he turned back around in his chair. He shoved the rest of his breakfast in his mouth, taking a deep swill of coffee to chase it down.

The nurses on the corridor looked at the pair of them in surprise, and Cooper even nodded to a couple as they strode along the corridor. Rita came out of the kitchen with a bunch of menu sheets in her hand, doing a double-take at the pair. She smiled at Kate. 'Taking old grumpy guts for a walk? Good for you!'

Kate waved at her, her face red and shiny from the

exertion of pushing him so fast. Cooper laughed then, a lazy low rumble and Kate realised he wasn't angry any more.

'That's right, Rita, a nice romantic walk,' he quipped, even turning to give Kate a wink. Kate smiled for Rita's benefit as they passed, then leant in towards Cooper's ear. She ignored the jolt she felt as her lips brush his ear, and whispered to him, 'You do that again, Captain, and I will poke that eye out.'

Cooper flinched at the contact from her lips and laughed again. 'Be worth it,' he whispered back, his stubble against her cheek. She abruptly stopped and pressed a button on the wall. The door opened, and Kate wheeled him in. In the room, Cooper saw Kate's son sitting in a chair by the window, staring at them both in obvious surprise.

Kate opened the window a little, letting in the fresh air from outside. Walking to the door, she faced them both.

'Captain Thomas Cooper, meet Jamie Harper. My son. Jamie, meet Cooper. Since you both insist on being stubborn, I've decided, just for today, to leave you both to it. So, I'm going out for the day, and you two can damn well amuse each other. Good luck!' she trilled, pressing the door button behind her as she went. She passed Trevor in the corridor, pretending to discuss lunch menus with Rita, as she headed to her room.

'Trevor, I'm taking the day off!' she shouted at him as she went.

'About time,' Trevor replied. 'Have some bloody fun!' he commanded. Kate gave him a thumbs up.

'And eat something other than salad!' Rita added.

* * *

Back in Jamie's room, Cooper rubbed the stubble on his cheek with an open palm. *She's got more balls than I gave her credit for,* he thought to himself, amused. In all honesty, he found himself attracted to her again. Looking at her son, staring at him blankly, he pushed that thought aside.

'So, Jamie, what you up to today?' he asked. Looking around the room, he was surprised that it looked pretty much like his: bare, impersonal. As far removed from a child's room as he would expect. He somehow had the feeling that this was more to do with Jamie, rather than Kate. He found himself wondering whether her mood this morning was about more than just his refusal to work. He felt a pang of guilt, as he realised how much she had to contend with. He spied a games console and a few games under the TV, all boxed up. Moving over to the box, he pointed at it, motioning to Jamie. 'Do you mind if I set this up?' Jamie turned to him then, looking him over with eyes so much like his mother's. He nodded and a faint smile appeared on his lips. Cooper smiled back and opened the box.

* * *

Kate was in heaven. She whipped her head from side to side as her body cut through the water. Breath after breath, lap after lap, she kept going, powering through the water till her limbs ached. Some girls shopped, some did lunch or the salon; Kate swam. She had started early on, when her parents were never around, paying for lessons herself. She took to it like the proverbial duck to water, and it was her go-to stress buster. Hacking away in the centre's pool, she felt the stress and anger roll over her like the water, splashing into droplets in her wake. Eventually exhausted, she sat at the pool's edge, dipping her legs in the water. She had missed the feel of the water – she hadn't been in since before being deployed. She made a silent promise to herself to try and fit it in, some badly needed time for herself.

Flicking her legs in the pool, she lamented the

state of her legs. Not much time for pedicures, or shaving for that matter. Maybe she needed to sort that out too, make herself feel a little better. Even her eyebrows were starting to look a little crazy these days. She didn't dwell on the fact that she had only noticed these things since working with Cooper. The two things were entirely unrelated. She just didn't want to give him one more reason to judge her. Yes, that was it. Bound to be. Looking at the clock, she was surprised to see it was nearly lunchtime already. She decided to go and face the music early, apologise and at least make sure both her son and her patient got fed. She could only imagine the moods they would be in by now, she mused as she went to change.

Heading to Jamie's room first, having put on a fresh uniform and tied her wet hair back in a tight bun, she steeled herself till she heard a sound so familiar that she ran towards it. Stopping herself at the door, she peeked around the doorjamb, and she couldn't believe her own eyes. Jamie was laughing. Actual, God's honest laughter, right from the belly, a boyish sound that she knew as well as her own heartbeat. He was laughing, his face bright, head thrown back. She looked to see what he was laughing at, and her hand gripped the doorframe. Captain Thomas Cooper was sat on the floor, game controller in hand, with a bandana she recognised as Jamie's wrapped around his head, Rambo style. The pair were playing a fighting game on the computer, and apparently Jamie had just thrashed the captain. She was about to go in, to say hello, to see if Jamie's smile would fade when he saw her, when she stopped.

'Loser!' Jamie shouted, laughing once more. The solitary word came out croaky, and broken, like someone getting their voice back, but it was there. The word sounded like a love song to Kate, and she snatched it from the air and tucked it into her heart. Cooper feigned being mad, adjusting his Rambo band.

'Loser, eh? I don't think so, kid – best out of three?'

It came again – the croak. 'Deal... loser!'

Kate grinned so hard she thought her face might crack, and she slid down to the floor, careful not to be spotted. Tears ran down her cheeks and she covered her mouth with her hands to stop a happy sob escaping. It was there, ten minutes later, that Kate fell asleep, bolt upright in the corridor, swept under by sheer exhaustion, lulled into slumber by the sound of her son.

An hour later, Jamie's lunch came to his room, and Cooper made his excuses, promising to come back soon. On the way out, he closed the door behind him and nudged Kate. She jumped, throwing her hands out in front of her in a chopping motion.

'Whoa,' Cooper said, as softly as he could. 'Steady on there, Missy.'

Kate lowered her hands, embarrassed about being caught asleep in full view. She wiped at the corners of her mouth and eyes quickly.

'Don't worry,' Cooper teased. 'I find drool and eye bogies a turn-on.'

Kate's face dropped, and she scowled and swatted at him when she realised he was kidding.

'Knock it off,' she said sulkily. 'I didn't mean to fall asleep. Did you know I was there?'

He nodded, offering her his hands to get up. She took them without question, and he yanked her up with ease. He tapped his lap. 'Yep. Want a ride?' He waggled his eyebrows flirtatiously, and was delighted to see her face redden. She pulled her hands from his as gracefully as she could, feeling pins and needles in her hips.

'No thank you,' she said politely, smoothing her hair back into place. He smirked at her and she pretended not to notice.

'What's with the ninja moves?' he teased, doing his own karate chops to illustrate. She swatted at him again, trying and failing not to laugh.

'Stop it!' she said. 'I was surprised, it's a reflex.'

Cooper laughed. 'Okey doke.'

She looked at the clock. It was gone one o'clock. 'We still have some of the day left, do you want to get lunch and then do some work?'

Cooper didn't really. In fact, just thinking about working his muscles today, after the pain of last night, made him feel sick to his stomach, but he didn't want to be mean to her again after that morning.

'Fine,' he shrugged. 'But I, er, have to take it steady today. I didn't sleep much last night.' *Why did he add that little gem? He didn't want her to know that!*

Kate's expression was questioning, but he said nothing. She nodded slowly, seemingly turning something over in her mind. 'No problem.'

12

Kate paced her room. It was gone two in the morning, and she still couldn't sleep. She didn't know whether it was the excitement of hearing Jamie laugh and talk, or the disconcertingly comfortable afternoon she had spent with Cooper. They had ended up ordering burgers in, and chatting far more than normal. Nothing personal, just chit chat: films, movies, but still – she had found herself relaxing a little. She had noticed how tired and drawn he looked though, and she had a suspicion she knew what the cause was. She was just trying to talk herself into action. Jamie hadn't spoken to her that afternoon, not that she thought he suddenly would, but he also hadn't thrown anything at her and had even let her ruffle his hair, so that was major progress. Thinking about how Cooper had helped her son galvanised her into action. Pulling her mirror off the wall, she left her room.

The corridor was quiet, the staff quarters filled with empty rooms or sleeping people. Here if you weren't on shift, a lot of the time you were in your room, catching up on your sleep or researching some paper or another. She walked towards Cooper's room, looking in on Jamie on the way. He was fast asleep, his hair sticking up in tufts from under the duvet. She dropped a kiss on his forehead, before leaving and going to Cooper's room. She hesitated here. The door was closed, but there was a light under the door. She held her breath and knocked once. Nothing. She tried again, a little harder this time, hoping to God she wouldn't wake him if he was getting some much needed sleep. She heard a wail, a low grumble, and decided to enter. The light from the corridor bathed the room in light, and she realised that the light under the door was coming from the bathroom. Knocking on the bathroom door, she waited.

'What?' Cooper snapped. 'I'm fine.'

'Cooper? It's me, Kate. Can I come in?'

'No!' came the reply, followed by a groan. The man

was in pain. Kate rolled her eyes. 'Cooper, stop being a dick, make yourself decent and let me in!'

Kate heard nothing. She was about to go get help when she heard the lock being clicked open. She gently pushed the door. Cooper was sat in the shower area, wet through with sweat, clad in only a pair of white boxer shorts. He was gripping his stump. Kate went to grab the mirror she'd left in the corridor, and locked the door to his room behind her when she returned. She came back into the bathroom, sliding the mirror in between Cooper's legs, till the mirror reflected Cooper's good leg, making it look like he had two.

He was in a bad way, his face red, eyes gritted. She reached out, gently removing his hands from his stump. He flinched and resisted at first, scowling at her, but she persevered and he gave in. His operation site looked good, but the skin area around it was covered in bruises. Kate pressed her lips together, fighting the stab of pain she felt for him. This had obviously been going on for a while. She glanced up at him, and saw his eyes were closed tight, his head against the tiled wall.

'Cooper,' she said softly. 'Thomas.' He opened his eyes and pierced her with his gaze. 'Look at the mirror, please. It will help.' Cooper nodded once and looked.

After a few moments his face seemed to relax a little, as his brain registered the fact that it was seeing two legs. Kate started to rub his leg tentatively. He looked at her warily, and they both felt the tension in the room. Looking away, she concentrated on trying to be professional. She could feel the heat coming off his body. It felt nice against her cold hands. If he found them cold, he never let on.

'How long has this been happening?' she ventured curiously.

'It's happened a few times, that's all. No big deal.'

'I can help, you know. If you just let me...'

'What's the point of that?' he retorted. 'Not going to get me back into service, is it?' His eyes flashed with anger, and her hands stilled. He noticed her flinch, and he grabbed for her hand suddenly. She jumped. 'Sorry,' he said ruefully. 'I didn't mean to scare you. It's helping, please don't stop.' She swallowed hard. He squeezed her hand. 'I would never hurt you. I could *never* hurt you.'

She started to massage him again. 'I know that,' she said, giving him a small smile. *I do know that,* she thought to herself. *In fact, he makes me feel safe. He challenges me, sees through my bravado. I feel calmer just by being around him. Which was selfish, given our history.* 'I hurt you though.'

She waited for him to make a comment, close up, but his gaze was on the hands massaging him.

'That's different,' he rasped. 'That was the job. I figure you have enough on your shoulders right now.' Her breath caught in her throat at his words. 'So, how does this work?' he asked, and she was grateful for the change of subject. A way she could offer help to him. 'The mirror helps the brain to centre again. Tricks the pain receptors into rebooting. If you can, wiggle your toes, it will help. I can get you some pain relief?'

He shook his head hard, drips of sweat dropping down his neck and chest. She reached for the rack and started to pass him a clean towel, then changed her mind at the last minute and wiped gently at his face herself. He flinched again, and she went slower, dabbing the sheen off his hair, his face and finally his bare chest. She noticed how defined his chest and arm muscles were. She could see them flexing as he shook from the pain. 'You should take some pain relief, it's too much to expect you to cope without any.'

'No,' he said softly. She didn't argue. She finished dabbing him and threw the towel into the corner of the room. She went back to massaging his leg, noticed that he was pointing and flexing his foot. His colour had come back a little.

'It hurts a bit less. It's helping.' His face sagged

with obvious relief, and her heart went out to him. 'Thanks, Kate.'

She was surprised to hear him call her by her real name, and she kept working to cover her own emotions at hearing it from his mouth. The way Thomas had felt from her mouth. How his body had responded to the sound. *Whatever this was between them, it went both ways.*

'We can sort this. The mirror will help, and we can do other things too, if you'll let me. Your leg looks good.'

Cooper snorted a little. 'Oh yeah, it looks awesome.'

She didn't bite. 'The wound has healed, minimal scarring. We could start to work on a prosthesis once the bruising heals.'

She let the idea linger, not wanting to babble away or make him mad. Especially when he was so... not vulnerable, she couldn't ever describe him as that, just... not himself. She finished off rubbing his leg and sneaked a glance at him. He wasn't looking at his leg though, he was looking at her. Reaching a hand out, he moved it to her face, his fingers brushing her cheek as he tucked a ratty strand of hair behind her ear. She shivered at his touch, and her grip on his leg tightened a little. As he pulled his hand back, he ran his thumb from the base of her ear, along her cheek. Not quite believing what was happening, Kate's lips parted a little and she didn't dare let the breath in her lungs slip free. Cooper was looking at her now, and her gaze met his, seeing her own surprised expression mirrored in his. He winced in pain, once, just as his thumb grazed her bottom lip, and it seemed to wake him up. His features changed back to the cocky exterior he normally sported, and she grabbed the chance to rock back on her heels, away from him. She stood, and giving him a quick smile, she went to leave.

'Kate—' he called after her.

'I'll just get the nurse to help you up,' she interrupted. She didn't wait to hear a response. That name again. Hearing him say it was like she had never heard it before. Twice in one night, after weeks of 'Missy' and 'Doc'. She had no idea what had happened, but she did know that after today, seeing him with Jamie, how his touch had made her feel, she had seen another side of Thomas Cooper, and she was intrigued. Just who was the real Captain Cooper? Was he all the versions she'd observed?

Giving instructions to the nurses at the station, informing them discreetly of what had happened, she went off to her room before any other surprised nurses who had seen her coming out of a patient's room in the middle of the night could ask any questions.

When she had safely shut the door to her quarters behind her, she looked at the nail on the wall where the mirror had once hung. Laying down on her unmade bed, she touched her fingers to her lips, where his thumb had brushed them. *What a day,* she thought to herself, as she fell asleep thinking of broken soldiers, mute boys and shattered lives.

* * *

The next morning, Kate was scheduled to have a meeting with Trevor, to discuss her patient's progress. To say she was dreading it was an understatement, but Trevor was too distracted with the news about Jamie to press her for any details.

'So, Jamie spoke, and laughed, I heard! That's amazing!' Trevor was jiggling from foot to foot in his office, and he was making Kate feel nauseous.

'Okay Trevor, calm down, I haven't had my coffee yet!' She laughed at him, and Trevor grinned all the more.

'And a laugh from you! Wow, the captain is really working his magic, huh?'

Kate flushed at the mention of Cooper, and an

image flashed in her mind of him looking into her eyes, his face close to hers, his thumb touching her lip. 'He seemed to get through to him, yes,' she replied reluctantly, hoping that Trevor would let the subject drop.

'Well, that's good, and since he's doing okay with therapy, keeping active, we can probably decrease your time with him a little, get you back on the patient rotation. I understand he has refused the prosthetics, so I don't think there's much more to do, unless you disagree?'

Kate wanted to disagree. She wanted to protest, to fight for more time with Cooper, but what could she say? 'I quite like him now, he's growing on me'?... 'I think I can get through to him'?... The point was, she didn't know that she could change his mind. And she did miss seeing other patients, having new challenges. So she replied, 'Yes, that's good with me.'

Trevor turned away from his desk to the filing cabinet at the far wall. Drawing out a couple of files, he put them on the desk in front of her.

'Okay then, Tuesday 1st, start seeing these guys. See out the month with Cooper, and then we will reduce the days with him to just Mondays and Fridays. I'll let him know.'

Ten minutes later, Kate was on her way to call in

on Jamie before her meeting with Cooper. Walking down the corridor, she made a pact with herself to try to give Cooper her all till the end of the month, when her new clients kicked in. She would work the weekend, make him work, force him to listen. He had got through to her son, she had heard Jamie laugh, a sound she had thought lost forever. She owed Cooper this time, and she wasn't going to go down without a fight. She wouldn't have this soldier on her conscience. She felt guilty about enough already, and it was time to stop. Work harder to chase it away. As she walked to Jamie's door, she wondered whether her motives were really as clear cut and innocent as they sounded in her own head. Walking into Jamie's room, she was surprised to see him watching television. He was dressed and sat in his chair, engrossed in his programme, and for a second, she forgot that the last few months had even happened. He looked just like he normally did on a weekend at home, his facial expressions comical as he followed whatever character was in a scrape on *Power Rangers* this week. He turned towards her, and she saw a slight smile pass over his lips, before he turned back to his programme. She sat on the bed next to him, folding her trouser clad legs under her, having slipped her hospital flats off. She stayed there for a good half hour, both of them watching the screen in silence. When she next glanced at the clock, it was time for her to go and meet Cooper, and she got up to leave. A small hand covered hers, and she looked up in surprise.

'Five more minutes?' Jamie asked tentatively. She sat back down, covering his hand with hers. Kissing it, she nodded. 'Five more minutes, baby.'

* * *

Twenty minutes later Kate pirouetted to the rehab suite. Walking in, she sat down at the table, savouring the fantastic morning. The usual bacon and coffee smell filled the air, but something was different. Cooper's face was pure thunder, and he was ripping into his bacon roll as though it was the spoils of a sworn enemy.

'What's got you so mad...'

'What's got you so chirpy...'

'Trevor came to see me...'

'Jamie spoke to me...'

They both laughed as they spoke at once, and the tension in the air popped.

'You first,' Cooper said, passing her a roll and coffee. She took them gratefully, her tummy grumbling in anticipation.

both can't seem to help ourselves when it comes to the other.'

His eyes darkened, and she felt it then. The connection between them, snapping into place like a live wire. 'Okay,' he said slowly.

'Really?'

'Really. I'll try. But I have some conditions.'

'Of course you do,' she huffed, making his green eyes spark.

'What can I say, I'm stubborn. I pick the place. We go out Saturday, all day. Will Jamie be okay with that?'

Kate was too flummoxed to even worry about Jamie being on his own for the day. How was she going to spend that much time alone with Cooper? All she wanted to do right now was put some distance between herself and her patient, before that live wire combusted and took them both down with it. She squashed her emotions down, reminding herself that this was her job. He was a patient. Those lines could not be crossed, even without all the other baggage they carried. 'He got a new game in the post this morning, I doubt he'll even notice I'm gone.'

Cooper smiled, heading for the door. She had never seen him move his chair so fast.

'Where are you going?'

Cooper looked over his shoulder and flashed her a

smile so intense that she almost bit her tongue as she drank her coffee. 'I'm going to plan our date with Trevor, before you back out.'

There was a closed door between them before either even realised that the word 'date' had been used. And neither party particularly wanted to take it back, so it hung in the air like a glistening dust mote.

13

Cooper looked green, and Kate could see his jaw flexing again and again as he ground his teeth. He looked dog-tired, his day-old stubble clouding his cheeks. She found herself once again wanting to look after him, and she squashed down the thought. The longer she spent with him, the more she realised just how complex a man he was. He was cocky, sure. Arrogant. Alpha. But that was just the shell. He'd broken through Jamie's shield in half a day, Rita thought he was a sweetheart. Even the nurses were warming to his humour under that gruff exterior. In combat, he was grizzled, but risked everything to save a child. He loved his unit like little brothers, fought for them. Laid down his life to bring them home. She understood his barriers, as he recognised hers. She could understand his moods, bear the brunt of his anger and his grief for a life lost, and still stand to be around him. He didn't flinch from her either. Her hurt, her pain. Her cold mask that kept her protected. He saw right through it to the woman she was beneath. They challenged each other, and she knew he felt comfort from her touch too. Their bodies called out to each other, settling the beasts stirring within them. She didn't want to fail him. She couldn't bear it if he lost himself to the dark. She wanted the world to see what she did, in those moments they spent alone.

She was terrified today. She could feel the pressure of the day upon her, what it meant if he failed. The man could walk, he just refused to try, and she couldn't work out why. He'd decided to live, hadn't he? This was a man that led others into battle, risked his own life to save his comrades and, from what Trevor said, never shied away from a fight. The reasons for refusing to try eluded her, but she needed him to try despite them. She was now fast realizing that her time with him was limited, and thinking about not seeing him every day gave her a knot in her stomach that she couldn't ignore.

It was Friday, and they had been working hard all week. Tomorrow they were out on a magical mystery tour for the day, planned by Cooper, and Kate was worried about the impact of today on their weekend. She was curious about what he had come up with, but she wasn't entirely convinced that they would even be on speaking terms when today's ordeal was over. Taking a breath, she gave him a tentative smile. When he gave her a nervous one back, her stomach flipped. She didn't pick at the reason why. They were in their usual room, the weights ignored as they sat looking at the expanse of prosthetics. She had done her research, had sent out for the best types of leg available to them. Eventually, Cooper would be able to have a different transtibial prosthesis for sports too, enabling him to do more. That was all in the future though, for today he just had to get one on and be able to live with it.

'You ready?' she asked, looking across from her seat at him, perched on the end of his.

'I was born ready,' he said with a wink. They both laughed, and his attempt at being a goofball made them both feel a little better. Standing up, she squashed down the protective, nurturing feelings she felt that made her want to hold him and got on with explaining the prosthesis to the patient, like she would any other. She was still babbling away ten minutes later when she moved to put on the stump sock. His hand covered hers and she stilled, shocked. He put her hand between both of his and without saying a word, raised it to his lips. He dropped a kiss on her palm, turning it over between his. She held her breath, hoping her hands wouldn't betray her. She could feel a flush enveloping her body, and she prayed that the sweaty palm god would give her a pass this time.

'For good luck,' he murmured against their hands, his voice thick with something that spoke to Kate deep in her gut. Looking into his eyes, she smiled. Her stomach was doing backflips and somersaults, and she was suddenly grateful that they had skipped their usual breakfast this morning. She was pretty sure she would have been seeing it in reverse right about now. Putting on the sock, they worked together to fit the prosthesis, checking for fit and comfort. Then, wheeling himself over to the balance bars, Cooper carefully stood up. Kate kept her distance, just enough not to crowd him, close enough to catch him if he fell. Or try to, anyway. In her current state, she was pretty sure a chiselled six-foot two soldier would flatten her. Cooper said nothing, besides letting out a small grunt. She could see the muscles in his forearms flex and quiver as he steadied himself on two legs again.

'Ready?' she asked tentatively. Cooper, red-faced and ashen around the gills, nodded, a single drop of sweat escaping his rather shaggy hair line and making a run for his stubble, which these days was more like a Grizzly Adams tribute. He eyed the walkway in front of him as though it were covered in hot coals, and Kate's heart caught in her mouth. *You can do this,* she thought to herself, willing him on. *Go on, fight. Do it for me. Do it for yourself.* He moved, taking a first step with his new leg. He shook as he moved forward, and wobbled as the foot came down to the mat. Putting his weight on it as gently as he could, he slowly lifted up his good leg, just for a few seconds, before setting it down again.

He did this again; three, four, five times. Raising his head, he looked at Kate dead in the eye before sitting back down in his chair. Kate didn't dare speak. She was waiting for him. Giving him the time he needed. He didn't say a word, and she knew he was processing. He was pale and flushed, and he started to head towards the door. She watched him leave but didn't try to stop him. He turned at the door, giving her a small smile. It hit her right in the feels. *God, that smile. He did it.* She wanted to run to him, tell him how proud she was, but she made herself stand still. Fists trying not to clench at her sides.

'See you later,' he said, and was gone. Kate sagged into her seat. He walked today. Big steps. When she was sure he was out of ear shot, she punched the air, letting out a little whoop of happiness.

* * *

Kate didn't know how to dress, and she was regretting not living in the real world for once. Before, she would have popped to the shop to pick up a dress or a new pair of jeans, but now, in her bubble of existence, she had a distinct lack of choices in the clothing department. She thought of her wardrobe at home, packed away, and she felt a pang for the simple life she had once had. One that had seemed so difficult. Now Neil was gone, and things were not how she expected them to be. Not even close. Funny wasn't it, how things seemed difficult till the truly hard times hit.

She had long since resolved never to shout at Jamie again. When Kate thought of her nagging, raised voice berating him for not picking up his dirty socks, or refusing to have a shower, she cringed. A guilt set in so deep, a guilt only mothers knew about. The kind that led you to their bedroom late at night, to smooth their brow, whisper, 'I'm sorry', and convince yourself that tomorrow will be a better day. Add to that a pinch of working mother angst, a dollop of 'I wasn't there' agony, and you had yourself a recipe for a rather feisty dish of blame stew.

The irony of everything was that now, Jamie was less likely to do the things that got her so mad in the first place. Things like flinging his dirty socks onto the carpet for her to find. Chances were, these days he wouldn't even bother trying to put any on.

'What's the point?' his eyes would say to her, and some days, she was inclined to agree. What *was* the point? Jamie would never walk again, never wiggle his toes like he did as a baby, never kick a football. So now, they didn't argue about socks. Kate no longer sweated the small stuff. Till today.

Today, looking at the rather frail looking rail that held her clothing, she was sweating buckets of the small stuff, since all she had was swim gear, nightwear and work wear, and everything seemed to be on the tatty side. She moved the hangers from side to side once more, as if a designer outfit would suddenly spring out in front of her, but all she was presented with was a couple of sturdy cardigans and an old Avril Lavigne tour T-shirt. Not exactly 'surprise day out' attire. She sighed, shoulders sagging. Well, that was it. Heading for the door to tell Cooper the day was off, she was confronted by Rita, who was standing in her doorway, hand out in a knocking motion. Kate jumped.

'Ooh, you scared me there, Rita!'

Rita batted her away. 'Sorry duck, just wanted to drop these off for you.' Kate noticed then that Rita had two clothing holders draped over her arm, and there were two shoeboxes at her feet. Kate flushed. *Did everyone know about this weekend? What did people think, exactly?*

'I don't understand,' she ventured hesitantly. Rita took her stuttered delay in response as a chance to push past her into the room, shuffling the boxes along the floor with one of her feet.

'One's for today, one's for tonight. They're all labelled up, so don't be peeking at the wrong stuff, okay?'

Kate nodded numbly as Rita laid the boxes and bags on her bed. She went to leave when Kate grabbed her arm.

'Thanks Rita, I really appreciate this.'

Rita patted her hand, smiling at her. Kate could see the crow's feet and laughter lines on her friend's sweet face.

'You're welcome love, but it's not down to me. I'll make sure Jamie's fed. Have a good time!'

Kate looked at the bed, confused. 'Who did it then?'

Rita winked at her. 'A little angry birdie,' she said, chuckling. 'Remember, have fun.' Rita looked as though she wanted to say more, but she stopped herself. Kate could see it was an effort for her, and once again she wondered what people around the centre were saying.

'But...?' Kate said softly, prompting Rita to finish what she wanted to say. Rita stopped, the door handle in her hand, the door midway closed. Turning back, she clasped her hands in front of her, and Kate swallowed as she waited to hear what came next.

'Kate, don't waste this chance. Remember, you did nothing wrong.'

'How did you know?'

She waved her off. 'Oh, I don't miss much, but that's not the point. There is so much sadness around here, such darkness and misery. Seeing a bit of light is a welcome thing. It's something to cling to, not a thing to be feared. You deserve to be happy. More than most, as it goes.'

Kate closed her mouth, feeling herself well up. The rebuttal died in her mouth before it made it past her lips. It went unspoken as Rita said something that made Kate's heart clench. The door closing with a click sounded like a parting shot in the quiet of the room.

'Life is for living Kate, no one knows that more than Thomas. Remind him.'

Kate ran her fingers through her hair and walked over to the bed. The top clothes bag said 'Saturday day' on it, and there was a matching label on the shoebox nearby. Taking a breath, she opened the bag.

* * *

Three hours later, Kate sat with her back against a man. They were squashed up tight, her quivering back pressed up against his broad chest. She could hear her heartbeat in her head, it pounded from her ears. *Boom, boom, boom, boom.* She tried to run her tongue along her lips to wet them, but it was so dry it rasped along them instead, and she swallowed hard. She felt him squeeze her arm from behind her and point his finger in front of her. She followed where he was pointing and saw Cooper grinning at her. She couldn't believe she was doing this and what was worse, that Jamie would be there, watching. He had been positively delirious when they had set off in the minibus that morning. She smiled despite herself as she thought of her son, giggling and teasing her on the journey to the air strip. Captain bloody Thomas Cooper had only gone and arranged a tandem skydive for them. She couldn't say no and he knew it, which was precisely why he was grinning at her now from behind his frog goggles. She could throw him out of the plane with her bare hands right now, but since he was strapped to the other instructor, she restrained herself. Instead, she settled for a sarcastic grin and flipping him the finger. Of course, he just laughed harder.

When she had opened the first clothing bag, she had been confronted with a pair of jeans and a white T-shirt. Comfy, but smart. The shoebox contained a pair of bright trainers, again trendy, modern and functional. She had guessed at something sporty, it was Cooper after all. She hardly expected an afternoon at the spa or a pottery class, but this was something else. Trevor had even sponsored the dive, so the veterans' fund would be happy. She had no wiggle room to get out of it, and with Jamie being sat in the van ready to tag along, her fate was sealed. So here she was; after training that had terrified her to her very core, she was sat in a plane up in the air, strapped to a man who was so warm and comforting she wanted to straddle him for dear life, to escape what was coming. Final checks were being made, the path was set, and Cooper and Micky, his tandem, were moving to the now open doorway of the plane. As Kevin, her straddle-ee moved closer to them, Kate looked down at her feet, willing them to respond to her request, even as her own brain screamed at her to curl into a ball.

The wind and the sound of the engine filled her ears with white noise, and she kept trying to swallow, to spread whatever moisture was left around her mouth. Kevin squeezed her arm, showing her the signal that they were nearly ready. Cooper's voice cut through the wall of sound, and she looked up at him. His eyes caught her in their grasp, and for a second, everything stopped. His gaze told her so much, and she nodded in response. He nodded back and then he was gone. She half-ran to the door, leaning over the edge to watch them fall. Kevin jolted behind her, surprised at her sudden movement.

'Steady,' he chuckled, and then they were watching the plane fall away. She had no breath. The urge to panic was immense, and she had to really concentrate on trying to breathe, to not panic and black out. She was suddenly grateful for the rather scary training they had done. It had been like a birthing class – teaching you how to breathe, to cope when the world span out of control. She thought again of those eyes, and she took a breath and opened her own. The plane was a dot now, as they fell through the clouds. She wiggled her head and caught sight of Cooper. He looked so alive, whooping and waving his limbs around as he laughed with Micky. He looked up at her as they came level.

'Hey Missy, we're flying!'

Kate laughed out loud, letting rip a whoop of her own. She had never felt so alive, so free. She laughed at herself, up in the air, away from the dry air at the centre. As they floated down to the ground, she felt someone grasp her fingers. Looking across, she squeezed Cooper's hand back, and then they were gone, separate but together in their adventure. As the ground came up to meet them, Kate still had his hand on her mind. Even through her glove, she could still feel the heat of his touch.

* * *

Later that day, Kate had settled Jamie back into his room. She had never seen him so cheerful, so excited, not since before the accident. He was so proud of his mum doing a sky dive, he'd even been willing to talk to her, but that was short-lived. When he returned to the centre, his mood dulled a little, and Kate knew just how he was feeling. Coming back to the centre after the day out brought home just how much things had changed. She had made a decision, and now she just had to have the strength to pull the trigger. Things had to change; this limbo they were living in had to stop. Heading back to her room, she passed Trevor on the corridor.

'Kate, how did your day out go— ow!' He rubbed his arm. Kate drew back her fist again and he cowered in faux fear. 'Okay, okay! I'm sorry! It raised money for the centre, what am I going to do? Say no?'

Kate moved as if to strike him again but pulled him in for a hug instead. 'Thanks,' she whispered into his ear. He hugged her to him.

'Welcome. Glad you had a good day. How's the patient?'

Kate pulled back a little, but Trevor kept his arms around her. 'Doing okay today. Doing better, in fact.'

'Good. Should be an easy transition then, when you see other patients too.' Kate smiled, but it soon dropped when she thought about her time with Cooper changing. It wouldn't be the same not seeing him every day, and he was the one thing that had made any dent on Jamie's depression at all. When she put her plan into action, she would need all the help she could get, and she couldn't pretend even to herself that Cooper hadn't featured in her thoughts for the future. She just didn't know how that would work, let alone in what capacity. Trevor must have sensed her discomfort, and he pulled her back, his arms gripping the top of her shoulders.

'You sure you're okay?'

She sighed and looked at her mentor. 'I'm good. I never thanked you, either. For the job, for helping with Jamie. I know I was a mess.'

'Hey,' Trevor shrugged. 'That's what friends are for.'

She pulled him in for another hug. As she looked over his shoulder, she saw something move out of the corner of her eye, but before she could look, it was gone.

'I'd better get changed.'

After saying goodbye to Trevor, she headed for her room. Her mind was buzzing with the prospect of an evening out, but she needed to put her plan into action first. Reaching into the pocket of her trousers, she pulled out a piece of paper. Dialling the number written on it into her phone, she held her breath as the call connected.

'Hello,' she said, willing her voice not to shake. 'I need to hire your services.'

14

Leaving her room later that evening, Kate felt like a
baby deer, navigating her way down the hallway on
her new limbs. The contents of the second dress bag
and shoe box scared her more than the first, and it had
taken her ages to will herself to get ready. Cooper had
told her that afternoon to be ready for 7 p.m., but she
hadn't spoken to him since, and it was ten past seven
now. The dress she was wearing was exquisite, with a
designer tag that had made Kate blush. It was a deep,
midnight blue, cut from layers of silk that clung to her
form. Kate was grateful that she hadn't quite gone to
seed since being there. It felt amazing against her skin,
and she had even managed to dig out half-decent un-

derwear from her meagre belongings. The dress was strapless, but fitted around her chest perfectly, not showing too much of her ample bosom, and the long skirt swished as she walked to the main doors.

Jamie was having a pizza and movie night with Rita, who stayed on site some nights to save herself the long commute. Kate wondered what her son would make of her dressed like this. She stumbled on her heels as she thought of what Cooper might say when she saw her, but she reached for the railing, steadying herself. Lifting her dress slightly, she frowned at her shoes. They were stilettos, the same shade of blue as her dress, encrusted with intricate crystals around the sides. She rubbed at her heel, unaccustomed to wearing such nice things. She righted herself, and half-jogged, half-limped to the main entrance as the clock on the corridor struck quarter past. She was never late, and she found herself anxious to see Cooper again. And then she saw him and her heart screeched to a halt, her breath seizing in her throat.

He was in his chair, sitting sideways on to her, looking towards the outside at the waiting minibus. He was wearing a navy-blue suit, the white shirt bringing out the green in his eyes. His hair was freshly washed, cut into a fashionable style. It suited him, and

Kate found herself wanting to touch it. She flexed her hands in reflex, tightening them around the tiny matching clutch she held, containing some money, a lippie and her phone, in case Jamie needed her. She looked again at Cooper, and locked onto his green eyes. She smiled, butterflies exploding in her stomach, and made to walk to him quicker, but his expression made her falter. He looked furious, anger evident in the set of his jaw and the flash of his eyes. He was trying to hide it, she could tell, and he eventually relaxed a fraction, returning a slight smile. She felt his eyes take her in, and saw his expression change again. She knew just what he was thinking now, and she tried to mask her own reaction of confusion. The want in his eyes was evident, and even though she didn't understand his mood, she took a little satisfaction from the fact that he obviously approved of her outfit.

'You're late,' he growled, nodding his head towards the waiting minibus.

'I'm sorry, not used to heels,' she replied sadly. She had hoped that they were finally getting somewhere, but she could see that the carefree man of this afternoon was gone again. She walked closer to him, and he didn't look at her, focusing intently on the doors.

'I'm sorry,' she ventured again, but he just shook his head.

'Doesn't matter,' he retorted gruffly.

They walked awkwardly towards the doors, and as she opened the doors wide for him, she noticed he had two legs. *Two*. He looked like a different person, just for a moment. She resisted the urge to squeal at him, and composed herself as he came past. He was wearing his prosthetic. As he settled himself into the minibus, the driver packing up his chair, she sat next to him gingerly. He didn't look at her, focusing instead on the view outside the window. She glanced at his feet, encased in matching black dress shoes, and wondered how he would look, stood up in his smart clothes. She felt a pang as she thought of him out in the world; walking, running, dating, living his life before serving his country had torn it apart. What sort of man was he, before? She caught the odd glimpse, the cheeky humour, the daredevil streak, but that was all choked now, wrapped in tendrils of anger.

It was getting dark, fetching shades of crimson and orange splashed across the sky against the remnants of the paler hue of the dying blue horizon. She clenched her fist and braved another look at him as they pulled away. His head turned quickly, his jaw tensing as he stared out of the window. Had he been watching her? His jaw twitched as if in response to her unspoken question.

'Are you at least going to tell me where we're going, all dressed up?' she asked, her words clipped. He flinched at her tone, and turning to look at her, the look in his eyes made the blood in her veins freeze. It was a look of pure pain, anger. She didn't know whether to hug him or run for the hills screaming. 'Cooper, what on earth is the matter?'

His lip curled in disgust. 'Boyfriend not tell you about the party?'

She frowned, the confusion on her face evident. 'What boyfriend?'

He didn't answer, his green eyes seemingly pleading with her to tell him something. She just didn't understand what. She could feel her face redden, and hot tears sting her eyes. The first night out in forever, and she was sat all dressed up, not wanting to cry in front of this beautiful, broken man. A single tear escaped as she bit her lips, and she wiped it away quickly. The driver kept going, seemingly oblivious to the angry exchange in the back. Cooper's expression softened, and he pursed his lips, blowing out a frustrated breath.

'Kate, for God's sake…'

'I don't understand why you're angry with me!' she cried, her voice quivering from the effort of reining in her emotions. Had Jamie talked to him about his dad? His wording had confused her. 'Neil has nothing to do with you!'

Cooper's jaw dropped. 'Who the hell is Neil?'

'My husband! He's not in the picture any more, and I don't want to talk about it! Who told you, anyway?'

Cooper looked stricken. 'You're still married?' It came out more like a deflated statement than a question.

'No, of course not. We haven't been together since I left for Iraq. He moved out the night of the... the night I got back. I haven't seen him since. The stupid bastard can't be bothered to deal with all the shit he caused. He calls Jamie once a week, if that. So no, Cooper, my "boyfriend" didn't tell me about any stupid party. And thanks for ruining a night I was really looking forward to.' She let out a frustrated growl, covering her face with her hands.

'I'm sorry,' he said after an age. 'I didn't know about all that.'

She rounded on him. 'No, because I didn't tell anyone.' Her eyes narrowed as she replayed his anger, his words. *Boyfriend*. 'If you didn't know, then what were you mad about?'

'Nothing,' he finally rumbled, turning back to the window. 'It doesn't matter.'

Cooper sat silently next to her for the rest of the journey. She sat there, shell-shocked till they stopped outside a fancy hotel. Kate recognised the place. She had been here before for conferences with work. They had a pretty impressive ballroom too. It would have been a nice place to visit with Cooper, but she knew the night was ruined now. She sat clutching her bag, staring intently at the back of the seat in front. She felt numb; she wanted to run but she didn't trust her legs not to betray her. The driver got out, grabbing the chair from the back. He opened the passenger side, putting the chair in position. Kate went to move, but Cooper's open hand covered hers, stopping her. He reached for his wallet, and pulling off a note, he talked to the driver in hushed tones. The driver shrugged good-naturedly and walked off towards the smoking hut, lighting up on his way to some service staff puffing away in the shelter.

'Are we going back?' she asked quietly, not trusting herself to look at him. He couldn't even get out of the damn car.

'What?' his reply came, softer than before. 'No, Kate, I would still like to go out, if you like. We're here now.' He sounded dejected.

Kate nodded, keeping her eyes focused forward. 'Okay. But I don't want to talk about Neil, okay? I've tried to get him to come and see Jamie. He speaks to him, but he won't talk to me, okay. He blames me for the crash I think, as much as he blames himself. Our marriage was over long ago, before Iraq. Before all this.'

She felt Cooper relax at the side of her, and she allowed herself to breathe a little. She was kind of glad he knew. It was nice to speak the words out loud.

She felt his gaze on her and flushed. He was looking at her, but she didn't want to see that look in his eyes again, so she didn't chance it. Her heart couldn't take it.

'So now you're with Trevor?' he asked, his voice sounding as unsteady as she felt inside.

'Trevor?' she said, baffled. 'No, of course not!' She laughed a little, the random thought amusing her.

'I saw you today.'

What? She thought back to the movement she'd seen when she'd hugged Trevor. Realisation dawned, and her head snapped to face him. 'The hug? Oh no.' Incredulous laughter tittered out of her at the thought. 'I was just thanking him. He's like a big brother to me, and I've been a bit of a mess with everything going on. Why didn't you just ask me?'

'What would I say?' he asked, his words soft. 'Nothing to do with me, is it?' he added. 'You're a free woman. I thought that there might have been something between you, that's all. I misread it.' He swallowed. Hard. 'I was jealous, actually.'

'Of Trevor?'

'I didn't like his arms around you. I'm sorry for acting like an asshole. I don't... talk about stuff like this. I never *needed* to talk about stuff like this, till I met you. You force me to think things I never have before. Feel things.' His jaw clenched.

'Well, you called it wrong, Captain,' she squeezed his hand. 'My marriage was over a long time ago, and Trevor's like family. We've worked together forever.' Her lips quirked. 'You were jealous.'

'Yep,' he huffed. 'I know I've no right to be, but I feel like I know you.'

She was about to answer him when he brought his hands up to her face slowly, stroking her cheeks with the backs of his hands. His touch did something to her, fired her up and soothed something in her at the same time.

'I keep wondering to myself,' he said breathily. 'If I tried to kiss you, would you let me?' His fingers moved to her neck, her collarbone. Each stroke was delicious, and she felt it everywhere.

Her breath was coming out in little gasps now, and she felt embarrassed about how turned on she was. A minute ago, she wanted to slap him, and now...

'Sir, is everything okay?' The driver was standing there, looking uncomfortable. They looked at each other, Cooper taking one last look at her lips before pulling away, releasing her.

'We're fine, and great timing, seriously.'

The driver chuckled. Cooper positioned himself in his chair, and held out his hand.

'Shall we?' he enquired. Kate noticed that he looked visibly rattled, and she knew that she felt the same. It gave her a thrill to know that she undid him, too. She put her hand in his, and the smile he flashed her felt like a lightning bolt through her body. She blushed, smiling back, and they started to head inside.

* * *

Having survived most of dinner with small talk about the food, the room, and the other guests, they were just waiting for dessert when Kate felt his eyes watching her across the table. The dining room was opulent to say the least, all chandeliers, white linen tablecloths and hushed music coming from the piano being played in the corner. Cooper had booked a table near the terrace, and the huge patio doors opened out in front of them, bringing with it a hint of honeysuckle from the foliage outside. The breeze occasionally brushed up her arms, and she could feel them tingling from the touch, as though Cooper himself were touching her with his gaze. The heat from their earlier exchange was still there, a little awkward. Like they'd slipped past what they were into something else. A thing that neither of them could identify. He was jealous, thinking Trevor was more to her. Hadn't baulked at her Neil confession. He took all of her baggage in his stride, and she wondered what it would take to truly rattle a man like this. She picked up her wine glass and took a long sip, looking over at him. He was still watching her, a look of pure intensity. Swallowing hard, she felt her face flush and inwardly cringed at her body's reaction to him.

'What's wrong?' he asked, his lips curling into a devilish smile. 'Feeling a little hot?' She grinned back at him and cracked up laughing. He laughed with her, and the tension around the table seemed to pop. He wiped his hand down his stubble, neatly trimmed now, and grinned at her.

'I'm sorry,' he said simply. 'It's been a weird day, I know.'

She tipped her head in agreement, and they both

ignored the waiter as he put down their desserts. The waiter smirked at them both and returned to his station. 'Third date, sweaty sex later,' he said out of the corner of his mouth to his waitress friend.

She looked over at the couple. 'Yep, that's rip-my-clothes-off-right-now tension right there.'

Back at the table, Kate took another large gulp of her wine. She felt it relax her, tingle her hard edges a little. 'It has been, very strange, and a big step forward for both of us, I think.'

Cooper drank from his glass, swirling the contents around in a slow circle. 'How long were you and Neil together?'

'One of your questions?' she asked, brow raised. 'Coming up to ten years. Ten years too long really. Neil and I were never exactly love's young dream.'

'Well, if he gives you or Jamie any grief, send him to me,' he said, his voice low. Kate sensed the change in his voice and narrowed her eyes.

'Why, do you think I need protecting?' she challenged, licking a remnant of chocolate off her spoon.

Cooper cleared his throat before answering, and she couldn't help but revel in how she affected him.

'No, but it doesn't mean that I don't get the urge to look after you.'

Her eyes went wide at his words. Cooper even

seem surprised at his own outburst momentarily, but his resolve hardened and he locked eyes with her once more. 'I know we have our own stuff to deal with, but I'm pretty much done trying to stay mad at you, Kate.'

'About time,' she replied. 'I don't want to fight with you either.'

'Oh, I like the fighting, Missy,' he said, his lip curling up, flashing his pearly teeth. 'I just want to explore the making up too. This place? There's an event here for my unit, among others. Some charity thing I agreed to before... well they decided to dedicate an award to someone I knew. I want you to come with me, as my date.' He hadn't taken his eyes off her, and she sat, spoon in hand, mouth open in surprise.

'I'm flattered,' she said softly. She'd loved to see him with his men. Hightower had almost broken down the tent to get to him that day. They obviously loved and respected him. It would be good to see that. Good for him, too. Cooper pursed his lips, looking away, but she reached for his hand across the table. Taking his fingers in her own, she brought them to her lips, dropping a gentle kiss on his knuckles. Her cool breath made the hairs on his arm stand on end. 'I would love to come with you.'

They smiled at each other then, and as she went to release his hand, he gripped it tightly. He motioned to the waiter with the other. He came over, casting a sly glance at his colleague as he sauntered across the room.

'Just the bill please,' Cooper commanded. 'And another bottle to go.'

15

The centre was a ghost town when they arrived back home, bottle in hand. Kate could already feel the stress of the place settle again on her shoulders as she walked down the corridor towards her room. Cooper hadn't said a word on the ride home, but he hadn't let go of her hand until he had to. He had walked out of the cab himself into his chair, unsteady still on his prosthesis but he made the few steps unaided. She wanted to throw her arms around him to congratulate him, but she held herself back, sensing what a big step it was for him. He didn't need to be mollycoddled, and she didn't want to belittle him. She was fast realising what a strong man he was, inside and out. How gentle and loving he was beneath the muscled, coiled exterior of the hardened soldier he presented to the rest of the world. As they neared her room, Cooper's chair giving the occasional squeak in the otherwise silent corridor, she could feel the nervousness between them return. Cooper had the bottle resting on his lap, and she wondered whether it was for someone, or just something to help him sleep.

'This is me,' she said when they reached her doorway. Cooper nodded, running his hand through his hair. 'Will you—'

She was just asking him what his plans for tomorrow were when she found herself yanked down till she was sat in his lap. He put his hand around her back to steady her and pulled her to him. Her legs dangled off one side, the wine stuffed down the seat edge. She gasped and turning to him, she could feel his breath on her cheek as he looked at her, their faces almost touching.

'Forgive me if I don't get up,' he quipped. 'I figured that you would have less chance to push me away when I did this.' He closed the distance between them and touched his mouth to hers. His stubble tickled her face as his soft lips caressed hers, and she sighed into him. He used her open mouth as an invitation, flicking his tongue against hers before deepening the kiss. His hand pressed into her back, and Kate felt the heat through her dress. They kissed slowly, deeply. Kate reached her hands up to his face as she kissed him back. When she ran her fingers along his stubble, moving down to his neck, he let out a low rumble from the pit of his chest and his hand gripped her tighter. His other hand came around till he encircled her tight within them. He broke the kiss, breaking away just enough to look her in the eye.

She looked at him and smiled. 'You are so beautiful,' she breathed.

He kissed her again, laughing softly. 'That should be my line,' he replied, dropping little kisses along her jaw line. She closed her eyes, enjoying the sensations, the feeling of his skin on hers. 'You are stunning.'

She giggled nervously, unused to the attention. She stole a glance around them, relieved to see that there was no one around to witness them together. He sensed her unease, and pulled her further into his embrace.

'Don't worry, Missy, your virtue is intact. For tonight, anyway.' He smiled ruefully, and she once again pulled his lips to hers. The kiss was tender this time, deep but light, full of meaning. It made her head spin.

'We have to be careful,' she agreed, pulling back reluctantly. 'You are still my patient, and I need this job.'

'I don't know what's going on with us, with anything, but I know now that this was always going to happen. I could feel it the first day we met.' His facial expression changed like a kaleidoscope; from happy to pained.

'I'm so sorry, being around me causes you pain, doesn't it?' She made to sit up, but his arm tightened around her body. He ran his index finger from the top of her hairline, down her cheek to her jaw, watching the skin he touched. Kate wondered whether he could see the line she felt. It was as though he was leaving an indelible mark on her.

'It did, at first, but you know what they say,' he grinned. 'What doesn't kill you, makes you stronger.' She frowned at his bad joke, but he ran his fingers along her forehead. 'I'm not going to lie and say I'm okay with being in this chair, but I'm here. No more frowning Kate, I meant what I said. You made me want to try. You actually make me get my arse out of bed on a morning, and that's something I never thought would happen.'

'I—'

He shushed her. 'No more talking about Iraq. Let's just take this a day at a time. See what happens.'

'I can do that,' she told him.

'Good,' he winked. 'That's my girl.'

16

Kate pulled into the drive of their old home and pulled up the handbrake. It was another mild day, and the lawn looked good, considering the house had been abandoned by its owners. She suspected that Alf next door had something to do with that, and she made a mental note to take him a bottle of his favourite tipple as a thank you. After all, buyers wanted something nice to look at, not neglect and dead flowers. The 'for sale' sign stood proudly in the front garden. After ringing the agent this morning, she had been surprised to hear just how many people had been to view the house. The agent was confident an offer would soon come, and it had spurred Kate to take the full day off. Rip off the whole band aid. She was hoping that today would be the last day she would ever have to see this house, and she had come equipped. Getting out, she lugged the boxes and bags from the back seat up to the front door. Taking a deep breath, she put the key in the lock. Ghosts of the past, time to be exorcised.

Two hours later, having changed into sweats and a large T-shirt, Kate was sweaty and covered in dust. It was amazing just how much dirt could accumulate in an empty house.

She had started in Jamie's room, filling boxes with things he wouldn't use again. Roller skates, his skateboard. Football boots, recovered from the accident. She had wept over those, sat on his *Avengers* bedspread. All the little items he'd wanted, cherished. They would never be used by him again. She'd never watch him play a game of football again, never cheer him on from the sidelines as he zipped by. They'd have to make more memories, new ones. Ones that would put the joy back into his life. But it didn't make seeing the things that represented everything he'd lost any easier. The boots were scuffed, ripped in places, but she couldn't bear to part with them. They all went into the box marked 'Jamie storage' with a red star marked on it. Red for 'open when ready'. If ready. She had hired a storage locker, a huge space in which to store their furniture and belongings until the next chapter began. She had a moving van coming at five o'clock and a hell of a lot still to do. She was ruthless once Jamie's room was all done. She had taken every belonging of his, and marked all his furniture, except his bed, with purple stickers denoting to the moving men that they were to go into storage. Jamie would need a special bed now anyway. She marked it on a list on the clipboard she had brought with her. She would give the list to the estate agents. They would have to pass it on to Neil. Anything he didn't want could be tossed or given to the new owners. After that van showed up, anything not packed up or stickered would be consigned to memory as far as she was concerned. She would only take what was hers and Jamie's, the rest was not needed.

She stickered her furniture, the items from her father's house that she would never part with, one of the television sets, a good portion of the kitchen appliances and equipment. She moved from room to room, boxing and bagging, filling the recycling and rubbish bins outside. She heard the noise of a lawnmower out front, and reaching into the liquor cabinet, she pulled out two bottles of expensive scotch. Neil had been saving them for a special occasion. Moving day counted. She smiled to herself as she grabbed them both, heading out of the front door with the rest of the rubbish bags under her other arm. Alf was mowing the lawn, one eye on her house, and she realised that he had probably been using the chore as an excuse to check on her. She dumped the rubbish into the bin, squashing it down as best she could and headed over. Alf stopped the mower and smiled at her as she reached him.

'You look well, my dear,' he said, taking her in. He seemed to realise what he had said, and he har-rumphed nervously. Kate laughed and touched his arm.

'It's okay Alf, we are doing well, Jamie and I. And these are for you, a little thank you for looking after everything.' She placed the bottles at his feet.

He relaxed then, patting her hand with his. 'You didn't have to, but I'm not going to lie and say I don't enjoy a quality tipple of an evening. Thank you. I am mighty glad to hear that you are okay, we both are. Sheila is down the shops again, spending our pension.' He chuckled at the thought of his wife, who was just as lovely as he was. Kate realised that she was going to miss her neighbours, and felt guilty that she was always too busy to spend any real time with them. 'No word from him, then?' he ventured.

Kate shook her head. 'I'm working on it though.

Just wanted to get the house squared away, it looks like someone will be buying it soon.'

Alf nodded. 'Well, I hope they're better at doing the garden then you were.' Kate laughed. Alf's face turned serious then. 'Look after each other. We would love to see Jamie too, if he is up to it sometime.'

Kate smiled at her kindly neighbour. 'I'm sure he would love that. I will call, once everything is sorted.'

He gave her a hug then, taking her by surprise. 'I'm very sorry that things haven't worked out lately, girl, but I am sure that the good things aren't done with you yet.'

Kate didn't answer, she was trying not to cry.

17

It was late evening when Kate returned to the centre, and walking towards Jamie's room, a box full of games and bits from his room in hand, she passed the kitchen. A waft of lemon floor cleaner attacked her nostrils and she grinned, knowing that Rita would be in there, putting her own mark on the place after the cleaners had knocked off. She walked in to say hello, and stopped herself when she saw Cooper sitting at one of the tables. He was laughing as he and Rita chatted away, their low murmurs not quite reaching her ears. The bottle of wine from the other night was sitting on the table. *He'd bought her a gift for helping. This man,* she thought. *So many layers to unwrap.* Rita was scrubbing at the floor with her mop, and she turned to look at her. Kate looked back guiltily. Rita winked, motioning her to come in.

'I was hungry, thought I might try and scavenge a bite.' She took a seat at the table with Cooper, deciding at the last minute to sit one chair away from him. She could feel her skin flush as he looked at her. Rita chattered away, filling the silence, but it sounded like white noise to Kate. She couldn't take her eyes away from his. Rita's voice faded into the background, and Kate heard the faint noise of the refrigerator door closing before Rita left the room.

'She'll love you, giving her some work to do,' Cooper said, his soft but masculine tones feeling like a salve, smoothing over her battle wounded skin.

'Glad I made someone happy. I forgot to eat,' she said ruefully, taking his half-drunk cup of coffee into her hands. His mouth twitched at her gesture, and she eyed him over the rim of the mug as she drank. Taking two huge gulps, she offered him it back, but he waved her away.

'Looks like you need it more than me. Bad day?'

She finished off the coffee, holding the still warm cup close to her chest. 'Hard, but good in the long run, I think. I packed up the old house. It should be sold soon. You?'

He winced and looking at the kitchen door, lowered his voice to a whisper. 'I was asked to leave the gym today, apparently my mood was scaring people.'

Kate laughed. 'So, people are finally seeing the annoying Captain I know and—' She stopped herself from finishing the sentence, but she still caught Coop's surprised expression as she looked away.

He reached towards her, and she held out the cup by mistake. He took it from her and put it aside on the table. Touching her fingers with his, he smiled. 'Growing on you, am I?'

Kate blushed and swatted him away. He dodged her deftly and tightened his grip on her fingers, holding her hand between his. She could feel the roughness of her skin against hers, and she squeezed his hand. 'I guess you are. Why were you in a mood?'

'Frustration,' he replied simply. 'I've had enough of living like this, and I have decided that things have to change. I think we need to step up the work with the time we have, and I wanted to ask if you wanted to go on another date with me, before the dinner.' He kept his green eyes focused on hers, and without even considering anything, she whispered 'yes'. He grinned and started to lean towards her when Rita swept back in, a large tray balanced on top of her nimble hands.

'So, did you have a good day off Kate?'

Kate thought of the tribulations of the day, and looked again at Cooper, who was looking at her with concern. 'Not bad,' she said, 'I cleaned out my house, put all our stuff into storage.' Cooper said nothing, a myriad of emotions crossing his features, and she squeezed him again in response.

'Ooh,' Rita exclaimed, arranging plates and bowls of goodies from her tray onto the table. 'That sounds like a novel, not a day! No wonder you're hungry!'

Kate used her free hand to grab a ham sandwich, not wanting to break the contact with Cooper's hands. He made no move to get any food. Rita emptied the tray and moved on to cleaning the next room, looking back at the pair as she left the kitchen. She had seen a lot of things over the years, working in various kitchens, and she knew what was going on here.

Kate wanted to scoff the sandwich straight down, being so hungry, but she wasn't ready to let the man before her watch her eat like a pig. She took her time and reached for another. His stomach growled, and she looked at him in shock. 'Hungry?'

'Yep,' he said, smirking. 'But no food is worth letting your hands go. I would starve to death first.'

'For a hand touch?' she asked, teasing.

'To start with,' he countered, waggling his eyebrows comically. She put the sandwich to his lips, and he ripped off a chunk with his teeth, making her laugh. His eyes rolled back. 'Man, Rita makes a mean sandwich,' he said, moaning with pleasure. Kate nodded in agreement, taking a large bite herself.

Finishing off the food, Kate feeding him morsels till they were both full. She sighed with contentment, happy to sit with him, feeling the calm from his touch wash over her.

'Where did you go?' Cooper asked, his green eyes boring right into hers.

'I was thinking how nice the silence was, how comfortable we are with each other.'

'It must have been hard, packing up the house. I've always sort of moved around. Packed light.'

'It's just stuff,' she shrugged. 'To be honest, that house hadn't been a home for me in a long time. I've got some great memories, but they're mostly of Jamie.'

'You'll make new ones. There's plenty of time.' He took one of his hands away, and he patted his lap. 'Come sit with me.'

She didn't hesitate and walked around the table to him. He pulled her onto him, lifting her legs up to dangle over one side of the chair. 'Best seat in the house,' he quipped, his mouth inches from her own. She could smell his aftershave, and something else, something inherently sweet. She was about to ask him what the scent was when he placed both hands on her cheeks and pulled her to him. His kiss was urgent but restrained, as though he had been waiting all day to do it, and she responded eagerly. She grabbed his cheeks and pulled him closer, a muffled moan escaping from her mouth into his. He groaned in response, wrapping his arms around her tightly, caressing her body with his strong hands. They kissed forever, lost in each other, till he finally pulled away. She opened her eyes, and looking into his, she saw the lust and need she felt mirrored on his face.

'I have to stop this Kate, otherwise I won't be responsible for my actions.' He dropped another slow kiss onto her mouth, licking her lip playfully. 'You drive me crazy, woman. I don't want to stuff anything up for you here.'

She put her hands around his neck, running her fingers through the dark curls that sat there.

'You're not so bad yourself, soldier. You're right though. I'm only your physio, but I think we should cool things till you're not my patient any more.'

He groaned again as she ran a fingernail down his neck. 'That's not helping. I mean it, Missy. It's been a while, and talking dirty while you run your hands all over me is not going to cool me off.'

'Maybe I don't want to cool you off,' she said brazenly. His eyebrows raised in surprise at her words, and his eyes searched her face. 'Why do you do that?' she asked, transfixed.

'What?' he whispered.

'Look at me like that,' she said, suddenly shy under his deep gaze.

He dropped another kiss onto her lips, before placing one on each cheek, the tip of her nose, and her fluttering eyelids. 'I look at you like this because I'm trying to work you out. You're like a puzzle I can't crack, and I don't fail to crack things. I look at you because I am suddenly scared for the first time in my life, and I don't like the feeling.'

She tightened her grip on his neck, pulling herself closer still to him.

'What are you scared of?'

He looked sad for a moment, and her heart went out to him. She could hear it hammering against her ribs, as though it were a bird trying to escape its cage to find its mate.

'I never wanted anything in my life, not like this. The army is my family, my home, and I never wanted for anything, never looked back. The fact is Kate, the more I know of you, the more I want, and I don't know what to do about that. I feel as if I know you, and we met in a fucked-up way. In a fucked-up place. I know all that, but I still can't stay away from you. It's like we're the same, you know. I can't stop thinking about you. I want to tell this whole damn place how much I like you. I don't know what's going on with your life at the moment, but I know you need your career. You love it like I did mine, and I don't want to be the thing that makes your life worse. I have a lot to overcome, and you have Jamie. I just want to be sure you know what you're getting into. I have no clue either, but I know I want it.'

Kate agreed with everything he was saying, but it didn't make it any easier to hear. 'I know. It's a lot, but I can't stay away from you either. When the house is sold, I'm going to look for a bungalow. Move out of the centre. I want you too, Cooper, but Jamie gets a say too. I need to put him first, and we can't start anything deeper till you aren't a patient.'

'So we wait,' he said with a kiss to each cheek. 'Till we get our ducks in a row.'

She moaned even as she nodded her agreement, touching her forehead to his in frustration. 'Trust me to get the squaddie with morals. I thought you guys were all grab the girl and hang the consequences.' She was only half joking.

He chuckled, a low rumble that vibrated through

her. 'Not forever, just till things are sorted, till Jamie knows about everything.'

Kate winced at the mention of her son. He had already been through so much; she had no idea how and what to tell him about today.

'And what about Jamie?' she asked him, deflecting her own thoughts for the moment. 'Me having a kid doesn't bother you?'

He shrugged. 'He's a lovely kid, we get on. As long as he's okay with me dating his mother, I am more than happy. He has a father, I'm not out to step on anyone's toes. I just want to see where this goes.'

He has a father. If only he bothered to come see him, she thought to herself bitterly. 'I don't see there being a problem, but we'll have to take it slow with him. He's lost so much already.'

Cooper nodded. 'This is what I'm saying; the last thing I want is to make things complicated for you two, especially when you're getting on so well. You were really close, weren't you.' He said it like a statement of fact, and Kate smiled at him. He didn't miss a trick. When, and if, Neil did want to come visit, that would present another obstacle to navigate. She knew he was hurt, blaming himself and her for the accident, but that didn't help Jamie. He seemed to be okay with just speaking with his dad on the phone, but for how long? They all had demons to face, it seemed.

* * *

Later that night, Cooper sat on the bathroom floor, mirror placed at the side of his leg. He was slick with sweat, having woken from a dream that he was in the battlefield, running for his life. The pains in his missing limb had woken him up, and it was the first time he was thankful for the pain. The look on Smithy's face as he lay in the dirt haunted him even when he was awake, and he wasn't sure how he was going to pull off the gala dinner. The thought of it made him want to throw up, and it was only knowing that Kate would be at his side that kept him from cancelling his attendance. One thing was for certain; he wouldn't be going there in his chair, not if he could help it. He wanted to walk in there tall, with her on his arm, not pushing his chair. He owed it to himself and his unit to walk in there showing everyone that although the bastards had taken one of their own, the men remaining were as strong as ever.

It was an odd sensation, having pain in a limb that was no longer there. Part of him had been cut away in the battlefield, and it wasn't just flesh and bone. He wasn't the man that fought that day, but the person he was becoming was someone that he liked, wanted to be. He was making friends here with the other patients, the staff. Hell, he'd done a sky dive and taken a beautiful woman out for dinner. He spent time with Jamie, had even shown him how to use some of the gym equipment. They'd bonded over video games, and he was falling for his mother a little more each day.

He should hate her. The Cooper from that day did. He'd despised her for saving him, for making the decision to save his life against his wishes, to turn him into something he didn't want to be, but now he was glad. He knew she did it for the right reasons, and he had almost made his peace with it. He needed to figure out his next move, sure, but he was convinced that he could do something he would be just as proud of as his career. He found these days that he wanted to stick around, see what happened next. He was adjusting, learning to live this new normal. But for now, all he could think about was recovery. Recovery for him, and the doctor and little boy who had become entwined in his life.

He focused on the pain, forcing his brain to register what he saw in the mirror. Leaning forward, he made a fist, clenching his knuckles together till they went white. He took a breath, and pounded down into the space where his leg would have been. His mind made his body flinch at first, preparing him for the pain that should have come as his hand connected with his leg. He brought his fist up and down again and again, making his mind register the fact that no pain was coming. He looked into the mirror to see the reflected leg, and he pulled it away. His pain dulled as his mind caught up with the reality. He had been doing this most nights now, and the pains were lessening. In fact, he had slept through for two consecutive nights, which was pretty much a record since his injury. He knew that he would have to keep training his body to accept what his mind struggled to see, but he was on the right track. He just had to crack the prosthetic leg, and he was on his way.

He had even been thinking about life after rehab, which was something he had never considered before. When Kate had mentioned moving out of there, living nearby, Cooper had found himself picturing them all living together somehow, but he wasn't about to put that thought into words, especially to her. It was far too soon. Too fragile. Even though it felt so right, he didn't want to rush anything. It had to be the right move, at the right time for all of them. They were all broken in their own ways. Healing together.

Cooper already knew that he would give his life for theirs, and they didn't even belong to him. Not really, though he wished it would one day be true. He sat there on the bathroom floor, knowing that no matter how hard things were right now, better things just might be around the corner. There might just be life after the army after all.

18

Kate's morning had gone well, and as she headed for lunch with Jamie, she marvelled to herself at just how different the other patients were to Cooper. Was it because of how she felt about him? The other patients were so different to work with, to talk to. When she was around Cooper, she felt more aware of her own body, her own feelings and reactions to him. It reminded her of when she was at school, in science class. The teacher would give them a magnet and a pot of what looked like fine pencil lead shavings. They would pour the black filings onto a white piece of paper, put the magnet underneath. Suddenly, the pile would react, take shape. It moved with the magnet, standing up, like the hairs on the back of her neck did when he touched her hand. From nothing, it changed into something beautiful, and that's just how she felt. Beautiful. Changed. She just had to get through the next few months, steer Jamie through the storm, and sail off into the sunset. Hopefully Thomas Cooper would want to be on the boat when it set sail. Every ship needs a Captain, after all. For the first time in years, she could choose what happened. Be truly happy, in every part of her life. She still had Jamie, her career. It didn't look anything like she thought life would post-divorce, but just maybe she could still pull it off. She just had to make sure Jamie would be happy too.

As she rounded the corner to the cafeteria, she found herself looking for Cooper. Jamie wasn't here yet, probably finishing off a session with his physio, which had admittedly been going badly. Although Jamie was talking to her now, he still sometimes eyed her with a look of distrust, and Kate wondered what her little boy was thinking behind those watchful eyes. Her heart sank a little when she didn't spot Cooper, but then, she shouldn't have expected to see him either. He had decided that keeping a low profile while she spoke to Jamie was for the best, and Kate had to agree with him. She knew her son liked Cooper, but as a boyfriend for his mother? Maybe not so much.

The truth was, since the accident, Jamie was a different child. He had every reason to feel and act as he did, she realised that, but she couldn't help feeling renewed anger at Neil every time Jamie lashed out in anger. Guilt at herself for not being there. Neil had guilt too, she realised, which was why he'd chosen to run off. He called Jamie, but he should be coming to see him. She wouldn't have stopped Jamie from seeing his father, but the accident was Neil's 'Iraq'. Both parents felt the guilt of that day, in very different ways. Not that any of it helped their son now.

Taking a seat in the cafeteria, she smiled as she saw Jamie coming towards her, being wheeled by a stony-faced therapist, George.

'Hi,' Kate said, reaching for the saltshaker subconsciously for something to fiddle with. Jamie didn't acknowledge her, his eyes cast down at his chair arm.

'Hi, Kate,' George said, his Jamaican lilt coming through in his deep velvety tones. 'Not a good morning for ya' boy. Two cups thrown at me head this morning.'

Jamie snorted and glared at Kate. She glared back, using her best mum scowl, and Jamie's face screwed up tighter, his gaze intensifying. Kate's shoulders sagged as she sighed. She didn't have it in her to argue with her son this morning. She just wished the moments of frustration would dissipate, and she could have more of him back. Looking at George again, she smiled her best pearly smile. 'Thank you, George, and sorry. I shall of course be speaking to my son immediately.' She emphasised the 'immediately' and Jamie tutted like the petulant pre-teen he was.

George laughed a low rumble and, putting the chair's brake on, started to walk away.

'No worries, man, last week it was three. All progress is progress, no matter how small the victory.' He laughed again as he grabbed a tray in the lunch line. Kate turned her attention back to Jamie.

'What's wrong, sweetheart? You can't treat people like that, Jamie, and you know it. George, everyone, we're just trying to help.'

He flinched at her words. 'I don't see the point in being nice, Mum. They make me work every day, for what? I'm never going to walk again, am I? You know that. So why do this every day? I wish they would just leave me alone. I want to go back to school, to my friends.'

Kate wanted to break down and cuddle him like a baby right then and there, but she held fast.

'No, you won't walk again, that's true, my darling, and I'm sorry. But you can't give up. You are not a quitter, do you hear me? This therapy is about keeping your body healthy, keeping you active, so you don't waste away in that chair. Your life is not over, Jamie.' Her voice raised a little too high at the end, and her son locked eyes with her. She spoke again, gentler this time.

'Jamie, I know that you have been through an awful thing, and that it's not fair, but we are alive, and we are together, we have to find some happiness. You will always have me, I will never leave your side again, till you want me to. And then I will be right behind you, cheering you on.'

'Really?'

The question surprised her.

'Of course.'

'You won't leave, like Dad did?'

The question almost felled her.

'No, never. Dad... Dad didn't leave you, honey. I didn't want to be with him any more, and I guess he's mad at me. The accident, well the accident upset him too.' Her eyes narrowed on his face. 'Do you not talk to Dad about this stuff?'

He shook his head. 'He says he loves me, and he's busy working but he'll come when he can. You're not going to leave again?' he checked.

'No Jamie, I'm not. I won't lie to you either. I will

always tell the truth, when I can. Okay? It's you and me, bud, that will never change.'

He nodded, and a real, honest to goodness smile lit up his face. She grinned back, hoping what she had to say next wouldn't wipe it away.

She pushed aside the saltshaker, reaching for his hand across the table. He was warm to the touch, and she squeezed his fingers gently.

'I have something to tell you,' she started.

'Is it about you and Dad, or you and Cooper?' he asked, his face neutral. Kate suddenly felt like a naughty teenager, caught by her father kissing behind the bike sheds, but she continued.

'Well, it's about both, but they're separate things. Dad and I are divorced now, the papers have come through. You understand what that means, right?'

'It means you won't be fighting any more.'

Wow. That felt like a slug to the chest. This poor kid deserved so much better.

'Right. Well, you know I went to our old house the other day, to get our things? The agent told me that the house is going to be sold soon, so I thought we should think about getting our own place. Separate from here. Somewhere you can move around in your chair really easily, just like here. A new home.'

'And will Cooper be coming to live with us?' he

asked, again, holding back no punches. Kate blanched a little at the question.

'Why would you think that?' she asked, realising that her son already knew more than she thought. She didn't give him enough credit for how grown up he was. She tried to tell herself it was only a good thing, but she knew his childhood had been accelerated far too much recently.

'I think he likes you,' Jamie said, reaching for the saltshaker as his mother had. 'I know he does, actually. I think you like him too. You aren't as sad any more.'

Kate glanced around the thankfully quite busy and noisy cafeteria, and was satisfied that no one was listening in.

'Well, Cooper and I do like each other, but right now we're just friends. Would you mind if we were more than friends, later on?'

Jamie shook his head. 'No, I like him, Mum. He makes me laugh.'

Kate flushed with colour and, getting up slowly, she went to her son's chair, kneeling beside him.

'When did you grow up, eh?' He grinned at her, and she savoured every second of it. 'It's still you and me, okay? Nothing has to change till you're okay with it.'

He nodded, a sly grin creeping in. 'Does that mean I don't have to do physio if I don't want to?'

She laughed, kissing him on the cheek. 'Nice try, but no. Let's get you some lunch, before George comes to take you back.' He groaned, and the normality of his pre-teen grumbling warmed her heart.

He was still eating lunch when Cooper came in, coming over to them when Kate gave him a little nod.

'Hey,' he said, pushing himself into the spot next to her chair. 'Good day?'

Jamie shot him a little grin. 'Yeah. Mum says we're moving soon, but I get my own ramp, and I can decorate my bedroom just how I want it.'

'She did, huh? That sounds awesome. How did physio go?'

Jamie's face was comical. 'It sucked.'

'Yeah,' Cooper agreed. 'It does suck, pal. Stick at it though, eh? Then maybe you can come to the gym with me.'

'Can I?' He looked to his mum for permission. She raised her hands, laughing.

'Hey, you're all grown up now. If you want to, I think that would be great.'

George came over then, and Kate could see he was steeling himself for Jamie's reaction.

'You ready to go back?'

Cooper leaned forward, holding out a fist. Jamie bumped it. 'You got this, kid. Go kick some ass, and I'll come play video games later. Deal?'

Jamie high-fived him. 'Deal. Bye, Mum!'

The pair of them watched him push himself out of the cafeteria, George's surprised gaze before he turned to follow him out.

'He seems brighter. Everything go okay?'

To her horror, a tear started to roll down her face. 'Yeah, it did. Sorry, I don't know why I'm crying, but... yeah, I think it's going to be good. He grew up when I wasn't looking.' She sniffed then, holding back a sob.

'Hey, it's okay! I'm here, Missy.' The use of her pet name, once so annoying, made her smile through her tears. 'I'm here.' Cooper pulled her closer, putting her head into the crook of his neck. One hand stroked her back, the other ran through her hair. He murmured something under his breath, and Kate didn't quite catch it.

'What?' she whispered numbly. He looked shocked for a moment, and shook his head.

'It's nothing. You okay?' As usual, he had a good read on her. Knew she'd be embarrassed at the show of emotion.

'Yeah, I'm good. I'd better get back. My patient will be waiting.' She pulled away from him, but he stopped her.

'Kate, I'm here. Remember that. If you want me, I am here.' Kate nodded, standing up. Turning around, she saw Trevor in the doorway, stony-faced. Knew he'd just witnessed them together.

'Dr Harper, in my office when you have a minute, please,' he said, his tone clipped, monotone before he turned and left. Cooper cursed under his breath.

'Looks like the cat might be out of the bag.' He brushed her hand as he passed her. 'Come find me later.'

* * *

Kate knocked on the door to Trevor's office. A curt 'come in' saw her walking into the room, fists clenched with nerves at her side. Trevor had his back to her, standing in front of the window behind his desk. Kate stood there, not wanting to take a seat till he spoke.

Neither moved. A strange standoff, Kate staring steadfast at his ramrod straight back. The door swished closed behind her, and he sighed. Kate was just wishing for an earthquake, or an alien abduction when he turned to face her. His face was closed off, not the friendly, happy Trevor she was used to.

'Kate, what's going on?' He pointed to her tear-stained face. 'Why were you crying?'

Kate huffed with relief. Maybe he didn't see anything. 'I am so sorry, Trevor, it will not happen again. I had a big chat with Jamie, I got a little emotional. I'll be sure to do it in private in future.'

'I didn't ask that Kate, I want to know what's going on? I thought you were getting on better?'

'We were, we are – I just had to tell him some news, I was just worked up about it.'

'And what news is that?' Trevor asked, his jaw flexing.

'Well, it's personal actually, Trevor.'

Trevor ran his fingers through his hair, sitting down on his chair with a bump. 'Personal? Since when do we have secrets from each other?' He looked genuinely hurt.

'It's nothing, really. Jamie is doing better. I really think he's turning a corner.'

He nodded, but the tension didn't leave him. A sense of dread ran down her spine.

'That's good to hear. I understand that you have been under a great amount of stress Kate, and I am here for you,' he met her eyes for a split second before looking away. 'I just have to question your choices lately. You don't speak to me like you used to. And as for your patients, I have concerns.'

Kate stammered, feeling the need to defend herself. 'My patients are fine; they get my full attention when I'm working with them. I'm a good doctor, despite my change in situation.'

Trevor held up his hand to stop her. 'I know you're a good doctor.'

He was going to make her say it? 'So, what are you referring to, then? I explained that lunch was an isolated incident. Have any of my patients complained?'

'Kate, no one has complained. It's you, you're different. And I believe your objectivity might have been compromised a little.'

'You're talking about Cooper.'

He sighed. 'Yes, and what I just witnessed went beyond a working relationship.'

Her jaw worked, trying to form the words. Her career was very important to her. She'd never crossed a line. She followed orders, worked to the rules. When it came to Cooper though, she couldn't quite help herself. He'd only been looking out for her in the cafeteria, but things had happened. Hell, half the people at the centre were aware of them. Jamie had worked it out.

'I won't need to work with him much longer. You could assign him to a new physio.'

'Do I need to?' Trevor checked.

'Yeah, you probably should. I don't want to cause any trouble for you, Trevor. I actually think I have a solution though.'

'Yeah?'

'I think you should put Cooper with Jamie. They respond to each other, it would still continue the work needed for both of them, and I don't have to be in the room.'

'You think they'd both go for that?'

Kate knew they would. 'Yeah, I do. They push each other. They already spend time together out of session. I can't get through to Jamie like Cooper can, and he's patient with Jamie. It cools his temper. Both their tempers.' She swallowed. 'They're going to be in each other's lives, Trevor. Might as well use it to our advantage in therapy.'

He looked at her for a long moment. 'I trust you to make the right decisions, Kate.' He smiled. 'Captain Cooper, eh?' He laughed. 'I never thought I'd see the day when that man was wrapped around someone's little finger. I'll make the arrangements.'

'Thanks. I have a session with him tomorrow. I'll let him know it's our last. Thanks, Trevor.'

He waved her off. 'You're a pain in my ass, you know that?' He was smiling when he said it.

'I know,' she grinned, heading out of the door. 'But you love me anyway.'

19

Walking into the therapy suite the next morning, she noticed that Cooper hadn't arrived yet, so she sat down at the table, looking through his file. She'd not gone to look for him the night before. They'd crossed paths when he came to Jamie's room to play games, but she'd left them to it. Satisfying herself with a short touch of his fingers in hers, a chaste goodnight. They'd been reckless, and she needed to keep her professional life intact till the dust settled. She saw that he had just had a routine physical check-up, and even though it felt a little intrusive, it was her job. She needed to know these things, even though it made her feel a little snoopy. His medical records talked of his scarring from the injuries to his torso, his amputation and mental profile, all done through the army medic specialists. It seemed that he had told them of his phantom limb pain recently, and discussed the fact that it was improving by using techniques from his physio, named as her. She smiled, thinking of just how far he had come, both mentally and physically. She flipped the page and noticed that Cooper had requested another check, one for sexual health reasons. The blood froze in her veins. Sexual check-up? She was just about to read further when Cooper rode through the door, a large box resting on his lap.

'Morning,' she said hurriedly, dropping the file on the floor in her haste to get up. Cooper wheeled over to her, quick as a flash, setting the box on the table. A waft of breakfast smells filled the air, but Kate was too busy scrambling to her knees to notice. He came alongside her, helping her to pick up some papers.

'Whoa, you okay?' he asked gently, shuffling the documents into a small, neat pile. 'Where's the fire?'

'No fire!' she squeaked. She cleared her throat, aware that an explosion of colour had filled her cheeks. 'Er... nothing's wrong, I was just checking the paperwork was up to date.'

He looked at her, passing her the papers with a slight frown. 'See something bad in there?'

She realised he was nervous. Was he embarrassed?

'No, nothing bad,' she said, in a falsely calm voice. 'Why, is there something you need to tell me?'

She searched his face for answers, but he wasn't looking her in the eye.

'No, nothing I need to tell you.' She nodded.

'Coffee's getting cold,' he said, turning away to the table.

She picked up one of the cups, smiling when she realised he had got her favourite caramel coffee.

'Thanks, I needed this today.'

Cooper shrugged at her, drinking from his own cup.

'So,' she said, suddenly anxious to fill the silence that seemed to fill the space between them once more. 'Ready to practice with the leg again?'

He looked her straight in the eye. 'I asked the doctor for a test.'

'Oh,' she said, wishing she could shrink down into her cup and drown herself in the hot beverage. 'Why, were you worried about something?'

He frowned at her. 'You read my file, don't pretend you didn't.'

'I did,' she retorted. 'I am a doctor though, so I used my discretion. It has nothing to do with your leg, so it isn't my business.'

He scowled then. 'It isn't, eh? Well, fine and dandy then, isn't it. Let's just get on with the session.'

Kate sighed inwardly. She had upset him now, and her questions about his request for some tests not only went unanswered, but they picked at her. She wanted to know so badly, but she wouldn't give him the satisfaction of asking now. And what if she didn't want to know? If he couldn't... perform, she knew it wouldn't be a deal breaker for her. This, between them, wasn't about sex. Not only that, anyway. She was pretty sure the man would be able to make her come with a touch of his hands on her body. Lust wasn't the only thing that bound them together. It was all her and Neil had ever had, she knew now. It wasn't everything, it wasn't enough for a lifetime together. If this was even what this was. They hadn't exactly named it. Still, it made her a little grumpy that their last solo session was marred by their cross words.

Slinging the clipboard onto the table, she walked over to the equipment area, flinging the rubber mats to the floor haphazardly.

'Now you're in a mood?' he asked, tussling with his prosthetic.

'Nope, it's fine. Like you said, we should get on with the session. It's our last one, anyway.' It was a cheap shot, but him closing down on her so easily had stung. They were still feeling each other out half the time, their struggles rising to the surface and butting heads. Cooper was in her face then, as he reached for her arm and whirled her around to face him.

'What do you mean, our last session? Did Trevor fire you?' His face turned to fury. 'I'll go talk to him.'

She reached for him, looking down at their feet. 'Cooper, you're standing.'

'Yes, damn right I am. He's not firing you over me!'

'No!' she exclaimed, turning her hands to clasp around his. 'You're standing up! You walked over to me!'

Cooper wobbled a second then, as he realised. His expression changed from anger to pure joy and he started to laugh. Kate laughed too then, and they both stood there for a long time, laughing like crazy, happy people, their hands wrapped in each other's. She brushed away a tear from her face, and Cooper pulled her other hand in close, wrapping his left arm around her back tightly.

'You're crying again,' he rumbled against her chest. 'I don't like this new habit of yours.'

'I'm fine. Happy tears!' she laughed through a sob. *He was fighting, finally.* 'I'm only letting you hug me because you might fall over if I don't,' she said playfully. He pulled her a little closer, steadying himself.

'That right?' he teased. She felt his breath on her face as he moved in closer. He slowly, deliberately, rubbed his stubbly cheek against hers, making her shudder slightly. He kissed the tip of her ear, the movement making her neck tingle. 'And what else would you let me do, to keep me on my feet?'

She was going to answer but when he rubbed his cheek against hers again, she couldn't stand it any longer. She turned her face to meet his and kissed him hard. He didn't miss a beat and kissed her right back. She wrapped her arms around his shoulders, pulling him in, but he didn't sway. He stood rock solid, meeting her passionate embrace with every bit of urgency that she felt. She wanted to rip his clothes off there and then, and she groaned to herself at the thought of stopping. Cooper mistook her grumble for a release of hormones, and he kissed her more ferociously. She took it as long as she could without boiling over, and then she wrenched her lips from his. He looked at her, disappointed, but seeing her as dishevelled as he was, he started to laugh again. They parted a little, Cooper again standing straight on his own.

'And that's why this is our last session,' she breathed as his look turned devilish again. 'I can't be kissing patients at work. I told Trevor I thought you should work with Jamie.'

'Yeah?'

'I think you're good for each other.'

He grinned at that. 'Sounds like a plan, and it solves me thinking about you naked when I'm supposed to be working.'

She felt her skin flush. 'Exactly. Once Jamie and I set up home, it will be easier. For all of us. After today, you are no longer my patient.'

'Then we need that date,' he said, the lust making his voice so thick it made Kate's stomach lurch. 'I have to get my Missy fix somehow, tide me over.'

'I know,' she said, trying not to pant. 'Tonight?'

'Tonight,' he agreed readily. 'I'll make the arrangements. Seven okay?'

Kate nodded. She would have gone at any time. 'Shall we get on?' she asked, brushing her hair back into place. He raised his eyebrows at her as he wiped his lips on the back of his hand.

'Sure, but get on with what?'

'Cooper!' She groaned. Looking down at his leg, him standing there, she had another idea. 'For starters, let's get some walking practice in. If you're going to leave the chair at home for your event, we have a lot to do.'

His head fell onto her shoulder. 'God woman, you're a pain in my ass. Anyone ever told you that?'

'It's been said,' she giggled. 'Now get to work, soldier.'

* * *

Dinner was lovely, and now she understood just why he wanted her to dress warm. They'd been driven to a small family pub on the canal, a homely place with tiny bookshelves and knick-knacks on the walls, a roaring fire in the corner. It was such a relaxed place, couples eating, families having meals together, a few groups of drinkers milling around. They ordered stodgy pub food, and Kate cleared her plate even faster than Cooper did. At one point she looked up from her food to find him watching her open mouthed. She blushed, taking another bite, this time resisting the urge to shovel it in.

'Want a trough?' he teased. She rolled her eyes, mouth full of food. He laughed when she gave him the V sign. She knew he'd been trying to get her to eat more over the past few weeks. She was grateful for the care. The calorie-laden coffees, the breakfasts he brought daily. The food was lovely at the centre, but her body had been crying out for a bit of something different than perfectly balanced nutritional meals, or the one salad a day she had lived on in the weeks after the accident. She made a mental note to bring Jamie here one day, when things got better.

'So,' she said when she finally drew breath. 'Is this the sort of thing you would normally do with your dates, take them to the pub?' She took a sip of wine as she sat back on the comfy sofa. Having finished their meal, they had moved closer to the fire, taking a bottle with them. Cooper had surprised her by having a glass with her. 'And wine drinking, I didn't see you doing that.'

Cooper sat down next to her, his chair discreetly put in the corner by a helpful waitress. His prosthetic limb was doing well, and he seemed more relaxed than she had seen him for a while, if ever. His shoulder brushed against hers as he got comfy, and she didn't move away.

'Well, first of all, I didn't really do dating, so I don't have a dating plan. And men can drink wine, I actually enjoy a glass now and then. Not when I am... was, serving, obviously.'

Something flashed momentarily across his face, a wince maybe, and Kate waited for him to come back to her, back to the present. He smiled at her eventually, taking another gulp of wine.

'So, no dating, ever?' she asked, both delighted and terrified by the fact that he was so inexperienced in this area.

'Nope,' he said, looking right at her. 'I have had my fair share of women, but you know the life, it's best to have no attachments.'

Kate ignored the uneasy feeling that punched through her gut.

'Till now,' he added then, putting his hand over hers. He ran his thumb over the back of her hand in lazy circles, and taking her hand in his, kissing her palm.

'You mean that? I mean, we didn't really have the best start, did we?'

Cooper pulled her closer to him on the sofa, putting his arm around her. She caught a whiff of his aftershave as he tucked her into his side. The warmth from his body made hers tingle.

'We didn't have the meet cute of legends, no, but who does? We've been through a lot together, and we know what we want. I do, anyway.'

She squeezed his hand. 'I saw the effect I had on you when we first met,' she teased. Her face dropping when she thought of the hate in his expression when he'd woken up. After the surgery.

He dropped a kiss onto her lips. 'That day wasn't a

normal day. My feelings since that day have changed so much, I wouldn't recognise them now. I just want you to be sure, before we do say anything else, that this is what you want. I'm not capable any more of being alone; I can do it, but I don't want to. You and Jamie are very important to me.'

Kate's heart leapt. He was answering everything that she had wondered about, the questions that had kept her up at night, the ponderings that she had uttered to herself. She wanted him just as much, and she felt relieved that they were finally talking about it. 'I don't want to be alone any more either, Thomas. I... feel safe with you. You calm me down with one look. A touch of your hand.' She squeezed his fingers with hers to illustrate her point. 'I wish we could have more time like this, just the two of us.'

As if conjured from nowhere, a driver walked in.

'Taxi for Cooper?'

'Do you want to go back?' He asked her when they were settled in the car, the street lights punctuating their journey home through the dark streets.

Kate looked at him in question. He looked nervous, his eyes were bright with emotion, and it surprised her to see it.

'We could spend the night elsewhere, that's what I mean. No assumptions, of course, but we could. You have the day off tomorrow, Jamie's tucked up in bed. We could just spend the night out. Go back tomorrow, when we want to.'

Kate looked at him aghast. She knew that the driver must be able to hear them, but she found that she didn't care. 'What about when we go back tomorrow? People will talk.'

'I'm not your patient any more. They don't do bed counts for staff last time I checked, and I have something to sort out in town anyway, they'll just think I left early.'

Kate started to shake her head. 'I don't think—'

'Exactly Kate, don't think. Are you in, or not?' He looked at her with such an expression of love on his face that she replied before she caught hold of any of the errant thoughts swimming around her head.

'Yes. Are you sure though? We said we'd wait, till I left the centre.'

He looked thoughtful for a moment, and Kate cursed herself for even giving him the chance to reconsider.

'I know,' he said slowly, 'but it's just one night. It might be our only chance for a while.' He rubbed his hand down his face and sat back in his seat. 'Maybe I was being a little impulsive.'

It was impulsive, but she knew Trevor trusted her. Knew that she had taken steps to end her professional relationship with her patient. Today was it. She wouldn't be on his case now, in none of his sessions. After today, they would only see each other in passing. The move was weeks away. She thought back to the file she'd read. Was that why he'd ordered the tests? To see if their love life would include... everything a man and woman could share together? She kind of wished she'd let him tell her the rest now, but she knew in her heart, it wouldn't matter. Tonight was about being together.

Moving closer, Kate whispered to him, close enough to feel her lips on his skin.

'Don't take me home.'

Cooper wasted no time. He instructed the driver to go to the nearest hotel instead, and to his credit, he did just that, with the minimum of fuss. Kate went in first, and booking a room, she sat in reception, waiting for Cooper to dismiss the driver and get his chair. He came wheeling through the doors and she walked over to him. He went to go to the desk, but she touched his arm, showing him the room key.

'I got it.'

Cooper looked annoyed for a moment, and she giggled a little, walking to the lift. He followed grumpily. They entered the small space and she laughed out loud when the doors closed.

'Don't be so grumpy! You can pay me half back, if that's the problem.'

'I can pay my way you know,' he said begrudgingly. 'I wanted this to be my treat.' Kate rolled her eyes, leading the way out of the lift.

'Good, because I have a son and a messy divorce to pay for. You can pay for breakfast.'

His mouth twitched, and he slowly followed her out of the lift onto the corridor. Once in the room, the door closed behind them, they both stood looking at each other. This was it. All those miles, all those hours, all those moments together... this was it.

20

COOPER

When the door closed, I had to catch my breath a little. I felt panicked, and I didn't want her to notice. She probably knew anyway, she always seemed to read my moods, good and bad. The truth was, I had been in many hotels before, with women hoping to land a soldier. Attracted to the uniform, the danger, or just looking for someone to rescue them. Some people think that it's us that are the skirt chasers, and we are, but we have to have skirt to chase in the first place. I never promised anyone anything. In fact, I was always honest to a fault.

Now, in this room with this woman, the woman who broke me down and helped put me back together,

I was scared. This would mean something, something much more than just a night in this room. One look at her made me realise that she was thinking too. I never thought I'd bare this body to a woman, but if it was to be for anyone, it had to be her. I was falling, faster each day. Scared to vocalise it and scare her off, but she never ran from me. She met my fire, my pain, till they melded together in one beautiful mess. I trusted her completely, and truth be told, I was ready to fight again. Not for the government, or for the safety of others, but for a life of my own. I wanted to be in her corner; hers and Jamie's. Putting up a barrier was something we both did, but now it was time to build our own, against the world.

I stepped up from my chair, slowly, and she watched me, not moving. She looked so perfect standing there, the sight robbed me of my breath once more. I steadied myself on my legs and held my hand out to her. She walked to me, and as our hands met, I felt the pull of her deep down in my gut. She reached out to touch my cheek, and I kissed her palm. She locked eyes with me and, not moving them from my face, she moved her hand down to my sweater. I watched her, transfixed, enjoying the feel of her touch on my skin. She lifted the material up, discarding it onto the carpet. She placed both hands on my chest momentarily before stroking them downwards. I sucked in a breath in surprise and her hands stilled. She looked worried, and I kissed it away. I could feel her hands press against my chest, so I stopped the kiss, but she grabbed hold of me and pulled me in deeper. Our mouths opened and I flicked my tongue against her lips. She moaned in response, and I felt a twitch in my trousers. She must have felt it against her body because she pushed against me harder. 'Cooper, can you...' She bit her lip, and it hit me. She'd come here, stayed with me without knowing if I could give her everything I wanted to. Everything she needed and deserved. That thought pushed me further into loving the holy hell out of this stunning, complex woman.

'Let's find out together, Missy,' I teased, reaching for her, taking clothes off her body as quickly as I could, till she stood before me in her underwear. She shivered a little, and I took off my shirt, wrapping her in my naked chest.

'You cold?' I asked softly. She shook her head.

'No, just nervous.'

I smiled at her then, grateful that this woman landed in my life. 'Me too,' I admitted. 'We can go back, if you like?'

She shook her head, dropping a kiss onto my lips. 'No, no more going back. Only forward from now on.'

I kissed her again.

'I love you,' I uttered, before I even realised I was going to. She looked at me, surprised, and in the moment before she spoke, I have never felt so exposed, so unprotected. I should have held the words back, waited. I was a patient man in everything but her. I held her tight, willing her not to panic, not to run. I should have known better. My girl was fiercer than that.

'I love you too, Thomas.'

I didn't need to know anything else. I kissed her hard, and she kissed me right back. I backed her up to the bed, slowly, carefully and she let me take the lead. Let me find my feet, take my own path, like always. I pushed her down so she sat on the bed, and I took a step back. She went to reach for me, but I held out a hand to stop her. I needed to do this. She had seen me before, at my worst, but I needed her to be aware of just what she was signing up for. Not as a patient, but as the man she might spend forever with. I undid my belt, letting my trousers fall to my feet. Kicking them off one foot, I removed them from my prosthetic and tossed them to one side. Taking a step towards her, I did the same with my boxers, before standing once more before her. She took me in, looking me up and down, pausing at the parts she had seen the least of.

'You are perfect,' she said. 'Come here.'

I shook my head. 'I need to do this as me, the new me.'

She placed her hands on her lap as a sign of waiting. *I didn't deserve this woman, but I was damn well going to earn her. Make her see that her words and actions, even the ones I had fought against like a foe on the battlefield, were worth it. Accepted. Cherished.*

Moving forward, I steadied myself against the bed as I took off my prosthesis, then using the back of the nearby chair, I stood before her once more. She smiled at me, an open smile of admiration, and stood with me.

'You never have to hide a thing from me,' she breathed.

'Back at you, baby.'

This time we came down to the bed together, kissing each other once more. We laid down and I looked down at her as I took her bra off. She shivered again as the chill in the air hit her, and I grinned as I ran my teeth across her collarbone. She sighed a little, breathing my name, and I couldn't hold back any longer. We kissed passionately, running our hands over each other as we laid tightly against each other. I knew she could feel me against her body, and she pulled away suddenly.

'Protection?' she said, pulling a face. Shit. I groaned as I realised I hadn't come prepared. I hadn't even thought about it.

'Sorry,' I grumbled. 'I can't believe this!'

We both laughed then, and she kissed me again.

'I am good if you are, Captain. I haven't exactly been doing this a lot lately.'

I nodded with relief. I was clean too, and it meant a lot to me that she assumed that of me. Another reason why I loved her.

'But what about...' I started.

She shook her head. 'I'm still on the pill.'

I dropped my head, rubbing my stubbly cheek against her neck as I thanked my lucky stars. She squirmed beneath me. 'No teasing,' she scolded. I felt her hand around me then, guiding me closer. I stopped teasing, let my fingers do the talking. 'Oh Thomas,' she whimpered, her head falling back.

'Do you know what it does to me when you say my name?' I growled as my fingers found her wetness. *All for me.* I felt like a fucking conquering hero. 'It does things to my insides. Makes me want to turn you on so damn much you scream it.'

I kept up my movements, finding her centre with my thumb and revelling in the way she jolted against me. She worked her hand up and down my shaft, making my vision blur. My head spin. As she placed the head of my cock at her entrance, thrusting her hips up to bump it against herself, she looked me in the eye.

'So make me, Captain. Give it to me.'

After that, I was a fucking goner.

* * *

Kate watched the sun rise through the slit in the half-open curtains as she listened to Cooper's heart beating beneath her ear. They had hardly slept, not that she was complaining, but she had to get back soon. She'd taken the day off to house hunt for a suitable bungalow for herself and Jamie. And Cooper, hopefully. They hadn't discussed it, but Kate knew that she wanted him with them. He loved her. Truly loved her, and when he'd said the words there was no panic, no doubt. She wanted to make them both a home, a better home than either of them had ever had, one filled with love and laughter, to give Jamie a home he'd adore. A place they could all heal properly, together.

She propped her head up on one elbow and looked at her sleeping partner. His usual frown lines seemed diminished, and a ghost of a smile played across his lips. He looked happy, and peaceful, and

Kate thought he had never looked so handsome. He looked a little pale against the white sheets, and she thought back to that day when his body was tanned and broken. She slowly traced her finger over his scars, the lines of skin salvaged and painstakingly stitched back together once the shrapnel was free. They were turning silvery white now, healing more and more as each day passed. She wondered if the beating heart she could hear was being healed by her, patched up with her love for him. He slept on his back, slightly twisted so that his legs were wrapped around her under the sheets. He was totally at peace, but she knew if danger kicked the door down, he would be ready to protect her to his last breath, and even though she would never admit it, it made her feel safe and protected. She had never got that feeling from Neil; she had felt like the stronger, more adult half of their pairing. What she felt now, lying in this bed, was a perfect match. She just hoped that the next few months didn't alter them. She snuggled into him further, half closing her eyes. One more minute, and then she would get up. One more minute, to savour this slice of time.

The knocking was insistent, and Kate scrunched her eyes up at the intrusion to her dreams. Trevor. That was her first thought. It was Trevor, knocking at her room door to tell her a patient was incoming. A flash of Cooper, naked, popped into her head and her eyes sprang open.

'Shit!' she shouted. She heard the door open, and as she frantically glanced around, the hotel room swam into focus, along with her bra, which hung from the mounted television. Muted voices were exchanged and then Cooper, clad in a pair of boxers, walked slowly back to her, wallet in hand.

'It was reception. We slept in, so they wanted to check if we wanted the room again for tonight. I tipped them to give us an extra half hour.' He kissed her, and she closed her lips tight. He faltered, pulling back, and she realised he had his limb on, and his breath smelled of mint.

'Scared of morning breath?' he chuckled.

She spoke out of the corner of her mouth. 'Mine, not yours,' she said, grabbing for the sheets to tuck round her as she headed for the bathroom. Picking her clothes up, he flicked her thong at her. She caught it, blushing, and grabbed her bra on the way past.

He blocked her path to the bathroom, and she looked up at him, flustered.

'No regrets?' he said, and she realised he was worried. She pecked him close mouthed, dropping the sheet. His eyes bulged as he took her in.

'None,' she said saucily. 'Half an hour means we have enough time for a shower too. I noticed a shelf in there, just right for sitting on.'

He broke into a broad smile then, taking her by the hand to the bathroom. She put her finger to his lips as they neared hers.

'I must just brush my teeth first,' she said. Cooper chuckled, and he shut the door behind them.

* * *

Later that afternoon, Cooper having left, Kate was enjoying a wander around the city centre. She had bought some new clothes for Jamie, and was now sitting in a coffee shop looking at bungalow listings from the estate agents. The lady had been really nice, not batting an eyelid at the long list of specifications that she rattled off at her. Some of them, one in particular, looked promising. The one she had her eye on had land with it, and Kate wondered if this could be put to good use going forward. It was just out of town, a large country-style bungalow. Just the ticket for their new life. Kate turned her phone on, intending to book a viewing, when her phone burst into life. She had missed calls, texts and voicemails. The centre number came up repeatedly. *Jamie.* Kate grabbed her things and raced to the nearest taxi rank. She punched the voicemail button and listened as she fired out her destination to the receptionist. It was Trevor.

'Kate, it's me. Listen, get back here as soon as you can. Jamie is missing.'

Kate's blood ran cold. The taxi pulled up, and she jumped in, ignoring the driver's cheery greeting. She rang Cooper's mobile. He picked up on the second ring.

'Missy! I was just thinking ab—'

'Cooper!' she screamed into the phone. 'It's Jamie. I need you!'

* * *

Kate's voice down that telephone line made Cooper think of the first day he met her. The urgency in her voice terrified him. When she told me what was happening, his instincts took over.

'Okay, I'm here Kate, listen, I am on my way to help, okay? Ring me when you get to the centre.'

Kate managed to pull herself together long enough to say goodbye, and he resisted the urge to tell her he loved her again. It didn't seem right, when they had only just told each other how they felt the night before. He would tell her when he saw her. When she was in his arms and Jamie was safe.

He rang Rita. No way was he going to speak to Trevor. It happened on his watch. Trevor wouldn't tell him a damn thing anyway. Why would he? Officially, Cooper was only a fellow patient.

Rita answered in her usual brisk busy bee manner. 'Can I help, my love?' Cooper could hear the noises of the kitchen in the background. The hiss of water running, the clang of pots and pans.

'Hey, Reet. Did you see where he went? How the hell did he get out?'

'I have no idea, the staff were all busy, and Trevor was holed into his office. His grandparents came for him, and he went willingly. It was one of the new nurses, she didn't know the background, and there's nothing in his file about him not being allowed to visit his father's family.'

'Wait, his father's parents came and took him?'

Rita's voice came across loud and clear. 'Yes honey, and he went with them willingly.'

He mumbled his thanks before ending the call to make another.

'Hightower, hey,' he barked out down the line, all his training taking over. 'I need an address dude, like now. Quick as you can. I'll text you the name.' He thought for a moment. 'And can you get his parents' too?'

Hightower didn't need asking twice. The man could hit a fly between the eyes from a mile away, a bit of tracking would be no problem. Ten minutes later, Cooper was on my way to meet Kate's ex-husband.

21

COOPER

Pulling up at the address Hightower had given me, I thanked my driver as he passed me my chair. I wished I could do this on my own two feet, but I just can't do it yet. I had some pride, falling arse-over-head wasn't part of my plan. I saw a car on the drive of the smart detached house. It was a nice area, not as nice as where Kate said she lived, but nice. Families lived here. The car was decent too, a rather sporty executive type. I bucked the trend with cars; being army born and bred, I didn't notice anything about a car other than the tyre width and whether it can take a hammering. Settling into my chair, I asked the driver to wait and headed for the front door. I checked the number with the text Hightower sent me. It was the right address, and it looked like a family home, not the home of a divorcé. Their house sale hadn't gone through yet. *You should have rung Kate.* He knew it would piss her off, but he didn't want to get her hopes up without checking Jamie was there first. I cursed under my breath, and knocked at the door. Heard a dog bark, a yappy little thing, and then the door opened. A man opened the door, but it wasn't him I saw. I could see Jamie, staring back at me from a man's face. My gut roiled. The man looked a bit surprised to see me, looking from me to the cab, back to me. He took in the chair and his smile faltered a little. He gripped the door a little tighter. *Coward,* was my first thought. Was this the man Kate once chose to spend her life with?

'Er, yes, can I help you?' he ventured, and I noticed him pull the door a little closer behind him with his free hand.

'Neil Harper?' I asked in a deliberately loud voice.

'Er, yes,' he said, pulling the door a little closer still. A quick flick of his eyes made me look to the living room, where I saw photos and ornaments on the mantel. I wondered who else was in the house.

I could hear a dog yapping its head off somewhere in the distance.

I kept my back as straight as I could, and looked

the guy straight in the eye. 'I'm here about your son, Jamie.' There was a flicker of recognition in his eyes, changing from panic to concern.

'Jamie?' he said softly. 'Is he—'

'He's fine.' *No thanks to you, shit head.* 'He left the centre today, with your parents. I think he might want to see you. I wanted to come to tell you, and to find out where Jamie is. He has people worrying about him.'

Neil switched from one foot to the other. The dog barked again, and I heard a door click shut. 'I told my parents not to get involved.'

'That's it? No questions about your son?' I countered. This sack of crap was getting on my nerves.

'I... I... who are you, anyway? Do you work with him or something?'

'I know him, and his mother. The question is, where the hell have you been? I know Kate wouldn't stop—'

The door opened behind him then, and he jumped.

A woman stood there. She looked like she'd just woken up from a nap. She was wearing a robe, but I didn't miss the rounded belly. If she was shocked to see someone like me at the door, she didn't show it. 'Neil, what's wrong?'

'Nothing, honey. It's fine. You go back in, put your feet up.'

'Are you sure? I thought I heard—' She was looking at me as if I might launch out of the chair and go for his throat. *No promises,* I thought, my lip curling.

'Look, as much as I would love to sit here on the doorstep and watch you two chat, I'm here for Jamie.'

Neil looked at the woman again, putting his palms out in a gesture of futility, and she glared at Neil as she went back into the house. The yapping continued. My ears felt like they were bleeding. Why the hell did people buy those groomed rats as pets?

He went to close the door behind him as he moved forward. I wasn't giving this guy an inch to wriggle. I just sat there, not moving as he manoeuvred himself awkwardly around my chair. As he turned sideways on, his ankle clipped the metal on the side of my footrest, and he hissed in pain through his teeth. I chuckled to myself, still not moving. Once he finally got himself out of the doorway, I slowly turned my chair to face him. The front of the house had a neat path all around it, and he stood kicking his toe against one of the slightly raised paving slabs. He wore trainers, the kind that a guy who didn't sweat for a living wore. Pristine white. I wanted to ask him so many questions about Kate, why he'd not bothered to visit his kid, but I didn't want to give myself away. The priority was Jamie.

'So, are you going to ask about your son?'

He looked at me, and I knew right off something had changed. This guy was angry at *me*.

'What the hell do you know about *my* son?' he spat at me. He leaned forward, speaking in hushed, angry tones. It reminded me of a daytime comedy I once saw. A couple were fighting around a sleeping baby, whispering 'screw you', and gesturing silent declarations of war.

'I know a lot,' I said, keeping my voice neutral. He needed to back out of my face, before I decked him. I clenched my fist against my stump. *Don't hit Jamie's dad.* It played like a mantra in my head, giving me the sudden urge to laugh. I lost my leg to protect pampered pricks like this?

'I know he misses his father,' I continued. 'Why won't you go see the kid?'

'I tried, in the hospital. I came back just before he left the hospital. She sent me away.'

'And since then?'

He looked confused.

'Question too hard? Did you keep trying? It's been months.' I could hear the edge in my voice, this guy was rubbing me up the wrong way. I needed to calm down. Find Jamie.

'I know it's been months,' he darted a look to the window, but the blinds were drawn closed. 'Look, I don't appreciate you coming here, talking to me about this. It's nothing to do with you anyway.'

I nodded at him, agreeing with him in a way. I wasn't Jamie's father, but I had been there. He looked at me blankly. The guy was completely out of his depth.

'Well,' I said, moving my chair back towards the waiting taxi. 'I'm glad I came anyway, not every day you meet a deadbeat dad up close.' I pointed back to the house. 'If that's yours, do better this time around.' His shoulders slumped at my words, and I felt a flicker of satisfaction that my barb had hit home. He'd already moved on. Before the ink was even dry on his divorce, he'd started another family. *Does Kate know?* She'd tell me that. Surely, she wouldn't have kept that from me.

'Will you tell Jamie I love him?' he said from behind me. I got into the taxi. I couldn't even acknowledge the guy. When the taxi was pulling away, I could see him staring at me through the blinds, back in the house. Hiding behind the strips of fabric. I pulled out my phone and dialled Kate.

She answered after two rings.

'Cooper?' Her voice was like a zap to the heart. I felt so protective over this woman that I almost asked the taxi driver to turn back.

'I'm here, Kate. Did you find him?'

* * *

Kate could feel the skin ripping away from the side of her thumb as she chewed on the area around her nail. A blossom of blood sprang up and she wiped it down her jeans. The foyer of the centre was mercifully quiet. She wondered just how many people here ran the other way when they saw her coming. She knew she was causing drama, but she felt like it was all beyond her control. What could she do? Her in-laws had taken her child from the place that he lived, without her permission. Any other parent of a patient would be angry that procedures were not followed. The trouble was, the only person in the whole place that knew of her situation was Trevor. She'd never documented her wishes. At least she knew now he was safe. She worried at the torn skin, pulling down her cardigan sleeve to cover it over.

A minibus pulled up, and Kate's whole body shook with relief when she saw the face of her son smiling through the window. She plastered on a grin and pulled the door open, running out to meet them. Jamie looked at her and she started to wave, but he turned away to talk to his grandparents before he saw.

'Hello, Kate,' Milly said. Roger busied himself talking to the driver, who was helping Jamie to operate the motorised ramp in the flash vehicle. A number of carrier bags sat on the floor, expensive clothes stores and games shop logos showing. Kate turned away, but Milly saw where she was looking.

'I hope you don't mind,' she ventured. 'We wanted to take Jamie for lunch, so we went into town. Bought him a few things. You can't take it with you, you know.'

Kate nodded at the woman. 'You didn't have to do that. I can afford to take care of my son. You could have called ahead. I've been frantic. If you hadn't answered when I called, I would have—'

Milly scrunched her nose up, readjusted her handbag tighter against her side, as though it was shielding her.

'I know you can take care of him, Kate. As we said on the phone, we thought it was okay to pick him up. The receptionist never said it wasn't, and Jamie was excited. I'm so sorry we worried you. Neil told us where you were living, and we wanted to see you both. You have done a good job, I know that. We just wanted to help. When you last called, we...' She swallowed, and Kate touched her arm. 'We just felt so awkward. Neil should have been there for his son, and so should we. He asked us to stay away, that it was easier, but we know now we shouldn't have listened.' Milly flinched as Kate squeezed her, and she smiled kindly.

'I'm sorry.' The relief of knowing Jamie was back, that he was okay, cut off everything else. They had been caught in the middle of all this. They loved Neil so much, had pandered to their only child. To hear them say they knew he should have done better, it made her want to stop punishing them. Jamie needed people, and seeing his face, so happy. This was a good thing, even though the timing could have been better. 'We shouldn't fight. For Jamie's sake, at least.'

Milly sniffed. 'Neil doesn't talk to us much about it, I thought it was your fault, that you might have been keeping him away, but Jamie says he hasn't been in touch with you. Only calls his son once a week.' She shook her head. 'I didn't know.'

'It's okay,' she assured her, as Roger and Jamie came forward. Roger was laden down with bags, but he set them on the ground and went in to hug her awkwardly. Kate let him, tapping him on the shoulder as though she was soothing him. Glancing at Milly and Jamie, she saw misty eyes and approving nods.

She wondered what Neil would think of this, or Coop. She imagined their reactions would be as different as they were as men.

As though thinking of Cooper had conjured him, a taxi pulled up and he got out. On two legs too. He stood there, as though he had all the time in the world, casually leaning on the open car door. He looked tired but utterly gorgeous. Kate's whole body responded to his presence. She hoped that the flame in her cheeks wouldn't be noticed by her company. He looked across at them all and smiled politely. The driver brought round his chair, and Jamie dashed over to see him.

'Cooper, I got the new Star Wars game from Grandma and Granddad, will you play with me later?'

Cooper sat in his chair and immediately leant forward and ruffled Jamie's hair. A move he did often now, a relaxed point of contact. Jamie giggled and they fist bumped.

'Of course I will, big guy. You had a good day?'

Jamie looked at his grandparents and beckoned Cooper over to them with him. 'Yeah, it was awesome. We went to a burger bar, and I had burger and chips. And pudding. We went everywhere, and I got some *Avengers* stuff for my room too. This is Cooper, he lives here too. He's Mum's friend.'

He presented Cooper to his grandparents grandly, with both arms spread wide. *Ta-da, my new dad!* He didn't say that of course. He might as well have, judging from the looks Roger and Milly gave each other. Kate could only stand and watch, picking at the broken skin by her side.

Cooper smiled easily at them both.

'Sounds like you have had a lovely day. Captain Thomas Cooper,' he said to them both, looking them straight in the eye while holding his hand out firm.

Milly eyed him coolly, but Roger smiled and held his hand out to shake his hand in return.

'Pleased to meet you, Captain. I'm glad to meet you. I have heard lovely things about you from Jamie.'

Cooper shrugged off the praise and Kate's heart skipped a beat. Modest, for a hero. The man had breathed life into Jamie, had given him his smile back, his laugh. These people owed him more than she could ever tell them. More than she could ever reveal.

'Hello, Mrs Harper,' Cooper said, turning his gaze to Milly. Roger gave her a look, and she uncrossed her arms and looking again at Jamie, she let Cooper take her hand. He shook it gently, nodding to her in deference. She seemed to relax a little then, and Kate could see her gripping his hand a little tighter. She reached forward suddenly, leaning down closer to him. Kate thought that she was going to tell him off, from her stiff stance and she locked eyes with Cooper as she moved closer to his ear.

He looked a little wary himself, but he flashed her a wink to reassure her.

Kate couldn't believe what she was seeing. Milly didn't speak to him at all. She threw her arms around him instead, hugging him tight to her thin frame.

'Thank you for being there for our grandson.'

Cooper didn't say a word, he just hugged her back. Roger came to her side and left the three of them talking as he pulled Kate further into the lobby.

'Has Neil really not tried to see Jamie? He rang us yesterday, and finally told us the address of the centre. We've not seen him since after the accident! He's acting strange, but he won't talk to us about it. We're going to the house from here, see if we can catch him after work.'

Kate shook her head.

'Roger, the house is being sold, no one's living there. Our stuff is in storage, I left Neil's things there. We've only spoken through solicitors. I'm sorry he didn't tell you.'

Roger looked at Milly, who was laughing with Jamie at something Cooper had said.

'This will really upset her. Do you know where he is?'

Kate had a good idea, but she wasn't about to do his dirty work for him. He hadn't even told them about the house.

'No, I'm sorry. I don't have a clue. The solicitor sent the paperwork to his office.'

Roger nodded. 'Then that's our next stop. We will help, Kate, you're not on your own. I don't know what happened, but my son should be here.'

Kate sighed, looking at her son who was now being wheeled around to the gardens by Milly, Cooper following in his own chair.

'I know,' she said. 'He should.'

22

COOPER

I never told you this, but I spoke to Hightower in the hospital, before I flew home. He came to see me, after my op. The op. He slipped through the net. I told the nurses and Trevor not to let any visitors in and at that point they were all bending over backwards in a bid to stop me complaining to the big wigs. You could hear the eggshells cracking and crunching under their tip-toeing feet.

I was kind of enjoying it, at least it distracted me from facing the truth of my new life a little. As you know, I wasn't a fan.

Hightower practically shimmied under the tent flap to get to me. He was so stealthy I didn't even see him until he was standing right in front of me.

I remember our conversation, even now.

'Jesus, stalk much?'

He had laughed then, a deep booming laugh that matched his huge frame. They didn't just call him Hightower because he was a crack shot sniper. The guy was huge.

'I came to check on you. I can't stay long though; the guys aren't doing well with the new dickhead in command.'

I laughed, but the pain soon cut off my chortling. Hightower's jaw tensed, but he said nothing. In our line of work, we know that our buddies have our back, but seeing them hurt, or worse, is unthinkable. When it does happen, we go to the mats for that guy, get to them, bring them home. Even if it's just their body, we risk our lives to get it. We know that we won't sleep, knowing that we left them there. We bring home what we can. There are lots of things we don't talk about. Is it a guy thing? I don't know. Till you, I never understood the importance of expressing how you feel. I kept it zipped up. Locked and loaded.

'Who is it, Daley?'

Hightower snorted, taking a seat in the plastic chair the doc had vacated. 'You wish it was Daley, at least the guy has chops. Nope, Simmons.'

'Christ!' I said, the pain worth the chance of a

semi-normal conversation. 'I would rather be shot in the face.'

We both laughed, till the pain in my leg started again, and I fell silent.

'You met my doctor? She's a real piece of work. You should ask her to lead you. She is properly blood-thirsty.' He gave me a look that kept me from saying more.

In our years of working together, Hightower and I have learnt to read each other so well that a look, an eye roll, speaks volumes to each other. He is the brother I never got to have in real life. In more ways than one. Sometimes, there are things thicker than blood in this life. Family is formed, not always born.

Sitting back in his chair, he folded one leg up and rested one ankle of top of his knee. His boot scraped against the side of the bed, brushing dust onto the white sheet. It looked all the darker against the clean cotton.

'You need to quit being a pain in the ass. I know what you're thinking, and you can't blame her.' What Hightower said to me then stayed with me, even though I buried it. Knowing what I know now, it makes perfect sense.

'Coop,' he said, fixing a glare on me that pinned me to the bed. 'She saved you for a reason. You can't blame her for doing her job. She's here to save lives, just like us. We're in the same line of work.'

I said nothing. What could I say? By that time I was too far gone in my anger. You know by now, I can be stubborn when I want to be.

'She's like you, and you haven't even noticed yet. It was like talking to you, speaking with her. Same stubborn attitude. This happened for a reason, Cooper. Don't give up.'

You see? Even then, people knew better than I did.

* * *

Later that night, Kate was reading *Harry Potter* to Jamie in his room. They had started it before she went away, and tonight was the first night since the accident that he had even mentioned a book. She had sent the nurse away, and she and Cooper had taken him to his room, where he had played Star Wars till his eyelids had started to droop. He was full of chatter after his day out, and Cooper matched his enthusiasm, talking about superheroes. Arguing, truth be told. Apparently, Cooper had an intense dislike of Thor. Jamie found this hilarious. Once Jamie was looking thoroughly ready for a good sleep, Cooper had said goodbye, saying he was headed to the gym.

Kate knew he was giving them space to talk. Jamie had let her bathe him and help him with his PJs. The small actions of helping her son get ready for bed almost made her weep for the past. She wondered how she'd ever moaned about the minutiae of life, the daily routines of raising a child. She'd always thought that she needed to blaze a trail in the world, but maybe she just had to look after her son. Help him live a normal life. Or even an extraordinary one.

'Mum, where's Dad? Grandma and Granddad kept changing the subject. I don't think they wanted to tell me.' Kate's brows lifted in surprise but she soon recovered. Maybe they did care about him. Enough to shield him from the harsh truth at least. Maybe they didn't know the truth. It certainly seemed that way today.

'Your dad loves you,' she said, settling him under the duvet. She ruffled his hair, smoothing it to one side with her hand. It was still damp from his bath, and she could see the drying curls of hair at the back of his head. He looked up at her from the pillow, and his little eyes broke her heart. 'He will always love you. It's just that sometimes, things are complicated for grownups. I promise you, one day it will all make sense. For now, I just want you to concentrate on getting better.'

Jamie nodded. Kate waited for him to ask something else, but he just sagged against the pillows. Kate got up to leave then, tip-toeing across the dimly lit room, but a voice stopped her.

'Mum, will you read to me? We have the books from our old house now.'

Kate was still facing the door, and she blinked away the tears that threatened to spill out.

'Sure,' she said, walking to the bookshelf. 'I'd like that very much.'

* * *

Kate hadn't been back in her room long before she heard a soft knock at her door. She was in a black vest top and soft white cotton shorts, her hair still in a towel from her own shower. She was sat cross-legged on her bed, bungalow listings spread out on the covers.

'Kate, you there?' His quiet voice sounded concerned. She uncurled her limbs, heading for the door. Opening it, she looked down to see him, expecting him to be in his chair, but her eyes landed on his hips. She flushed and heard a chuckle. 'You know, I have a face. You can't treat a man like a piece of meat.'

He had one arm on the door jamb, looking every

inch the cocky soldier she once thought him to be. Kate looked down the corridor beyond him.

'Someone will see me out here. You should invite me in.'

Kate looked at Cooper, but he just stood there grinning back at her.

'And they won't talk if I have a patient in my room?' She countered, stepping back to let him in. He strode in, watching her check the corridor once more and lock the door. The room was quiet, and the silence seemed to register for them both at the same time. Cooper looked around the room, settling his gaze on the papers strewn on the bed.

'I didn't mean to disturb you,' he nodded towards them. 'I just wanted to see if you were okay, after today. What did Jamie say? Did he ask about his Dad?'

Kate went to run her fingers through her hair as she composed the words and felt the towel. She pulled it from her head, fanning out her hair. 'Sorry, I look a mess. We didn't talk about it much. He has questions, and as yet, I don't know how to answer them.'

She folded the towel over the radiator, pushing her still-damp hair off her face. Cooper made no move to come closer, and she knew he was trying to be there for her. She hated that she had dragged him into this too. He had enough to deal with.

'Listen, Cooper,' she began.

'Don't.' His voice was so low she didn't trust what she had heard at first.

'What?'

'Don't. I know what you're going to do, and I am saying no. If you want to end this because you don't like me, then fine. Otherwise, the answer is no.'

He walked towards her then. Slow steady strides, as surefooted as any man. He put his arms around her, his warm skin bringing out goosebumps on hers. He lowered his face to hers, and stopping just before he touched his lips to hers, he asked again.

'Well?'

She could feel the heat from his lips near hers. Her whole body was warmed by his touch.

'It's not that simple,' she protested weakly. 'You have so much to deal with, and the whole thing is just a mess. You don't know the half of it.'

He released her, and she thought he was going to back away, but instead he bent down, lifting his trouser leg. She could see the metal of his prosthetic underneath.

'This is what I have to deal with. I can stand on my own two feet, Kate. The rest of it we can figure out. The only thing I need to know is whether or not you actually want this. All in.' He stood up, giving her a little smile before heading to the door. He pointed to the papers on the bed. 'Try and get some sleep, okay?'

Before she could form an answer in her own head, he had flicked the lock and slipped out. She locked her door back up and went back to the papers. She knew where he stood now, and she knew he was laying his cards on the table. In his own way, he was telling her he wanted them, no matter what. Today hadn't spooked him. He'd been there for her. Been nice to Jamie's grandparents. Looked after them both without passing comment.

She just had to take the leap with him. The problem was, it wasn't that easy to leap into the arms of a man when her arms were already laden with all the excess baggage of her life. She felt like she was dragging Neil along with her, a ghost figure in the relationship, and now Cooper had even met her ex-in-laws. Awkward wasn't the word. They didn't know the full story yet, and Neil was obviously in hiding. When it came out, the shit would hit the fan. Did she want Cooper to have to deal with that, too? He didn't do relationships. To be in one with her was... difficult. What you had was a Shakespearean tragedy in the making, not the ideal conditions for a tentative new relationship. It was when she noticed she was dripping water on the listings from her still wet hair that she gave in and went to bed. It would still all be there in the morning. Maybe it would look better then.

* * *

Kate rapped on Trevor's door, uniform on and hair pinned back. She felt like she hadn't slept, but she had done some thinking.

'Come in,' Trevor's voice came from behind the door. She didn't give herself the chance to back out and she walked straight through, taking a seat in the chair opposite him and putting the files from her arms into his in tray.

'Morning, Trevor, I've done all the charting up to date. I've a client vacancy now too, with Sean Wright being discharged, so if you have anyone, I'm happy to see them this afternoon.'

'Great, I don't have one today, but I will have a look at the admissions waiting list this afternoon.' He sucked in a breath. 'Kate, I am really sorry about yesterday.'

She waved him off. 'It's fine, honestly. It turned out well. It was a miscommunication really.'

'At least Jamie saw his grandparents,' he smiled, looking relieved. 'How do you feel about it?'

She bit at her lip. 'Good, but I'll feel better when

we are settled somewhere new. Me having a panic attack in reception wasn't exactly professional.'

He waved her off. 'He's a patient. You were a worried mother in that moment.' He pinned her with one of his big brother looks. 'I might not always agree with your decisions, Kate, but you're a damn fine worker. I don't think you should beat yourself up about it.' He steepled his hands together, resting his elbows on the desk. 'Do you think Neil will visit now?'

She sighed. 'God, I don't know. I wouldn't stop him. His parents are going to find out some things though. I think you need to know, in case it causes issues for Jamie.'

'Things like what?' he asked.

'Well, there's the accident. I don't think Jamie remembers. Neil was on the phone that day, do you know that?' His expression confirmed it was news to him. She'd been such a mess at the time, she'd kept it all in. 'Handsfree, so not illegal, but he was distracted. Not watching the road. It was his fault, and Jamie paid the price.'

'Jesus,' Trevor breathed. 'Thanks for letting me know. I'll get you that patient info, but in the meantime, go see him.'

She winced. 'He's in physio, with Thom— Cooper.'

Trevor nodded. 'I'm aware. It's fine. He's not your

patient any more, Kate. As long as nothing comes up, I'm good with you seeing your son.'

'Did I ever tell you what a good friend you are?'

Trevor laughed. 'A better friend would bring presents.' She laughed, heading off to find her two favourite men.

'Aww, I missed it?' The physio suite was empty when she got there. Cooper was on his way out, an open newspaper on his lap.

'Yeah,' he laughed. 'The new physio took him for something to eat. He worked so hard he put me to shame. Trevor find you? He was looking for you earlier.'

'I've seen him already. He said I could come see you. Jamie still wanting you to play with him later, or is he too tired?'

'I'm still going. I ordered some stuff online too, it should be here soon. It's a Lego thing. I think he'll like it. Thought we could build it together, it would make a change from just playing on the computer.'

Kate thought of Jamie and how he would be so excited to do that with Cooper.

'You like him, don't you,' she stated. It wasn't a question.

He looked at her, and his guarded expression dropped into a happy smile.

'I love him Kate, I love you both. That won't change. I'm here, I told you.' His words broke her apart, and she realised she'd been worrying about him realizing that maybe her issues were too much, even for him. The tears sprang to her eyes, and she couldn't hold them back. She dropped her head onto her arms and started to cry. In one move, Cooper had lifted her into his arms in his chair. He laid her across his lap and cradled her tightly.

'If Trevor comes in, this won't help fight our corner you know.'

She laughed, which sent her into a fresh bout of tears. He shushed her, squeezing her to him.

'I never had a family,' he said into her hair, softly. 'I was left, dumped in a side street. I bounced around the foster system for a while, but I didn't fit in anywhere. Not till I signed up. Then I had brothers and sisters, a family to die for. A unit that would die for me. It was all I needed. Till you and Jamie came along. Now I know what family is, in the normal sense. I would throw myself into the path of anything that ever threatened to hurt either of you. I know what I want, but I need you to be sure of what you want. Sure that *I'm not going anywhere*. Know all the facts. Something is holding you back, I can feel it. Till you figure it out, I'm here.' He lifted her head, wiped her tears with a white piece of cotton. Kate took it from him, looking at it. It was a handkerchief, with the initials TC sewn onto it.

'Rita,' he said grinning. 'She made some for Jamie too. That woman never stops, I swear. I think she adopted me.'

Kate wiped her face dry of tears. Her head ached from the sudden outpouring of emotion.

'What were you looking at when I came in?' she asked, remembering.

He flushed, shaking his head. 'Nothing important,' he said, but she could tell he was lying. She went in to embrace him, but grabbed at the paper and jumped off his lap. He was fast, standing to get it from her, but not fast enough. She saw the property pages from the daily paper.

'Are you leaving?' she asked.

He stood, walked towards her, and she noticed how steady on his feet he was.

'After the bash, yeah, I thought I might rent some-where close. A flat. I need to think about my next move, maybe getting some work. My savings won't last forever.' Kate felt a slab of something lying heavy in her stomach. *No,* she thought. *Nothing does.*

'Don't overthink this, Kate. It's nothing to do with what I said. I am here for you and Jamie, I just need to put things in place for me, that's all. My next steps include you.'

Kate nodded, and Cooper knew that she had closed herself down. *Damn it. The woman was stubborn,* he thought. He itched the stubble on the side of his face with both hands. The scrape, scrape, scrape of nails on skin and hair. 'Kate, don't do this.'

She looked at him, shaking her head sadly.

He wished he could tell her what he knew. That he'd seen Neil. Knew of his new situation. No wonder the woman didn't trust what they had. She'd been replaced so quickly by a man with whom she didn't feel a fraction of what she and Cooper meant to each other.

Meanwhile, her independent stubborn streak was screaming at her not to make another mistake. 'Don't you get it, Cooper? It's already done. There's just... too much against this. I can't fail again.' She gazed into those green eyes, wishing it was different. 'I don't want to take a good man down with me.'

23

Kate felt wretched after leaving Cooper there. She felt like she'd just walked away from him forever. Her past was dictating her future, and she was damn well letting it. As soon as she could break away from work, she took herself off to a quiet corner and dialled a number on her phone. Roger answered after two rings.

'Hello, dear, how are you and Jamie? It's lovely to hear from you!' His warmth and friendly easiness made Kate's stomach drop into her heels.

'We're fine thanks, Roger, but I do have a favour to ask.' She already knew that Neil's work hadn't told them anything. He'd called to tell her as much. 'Could you and Milly please come to the centre today? I thought you could have lunch with Jamie, and I need to speak to you too.'

Roger didn't speak for a moment, and Kate held her breath.

'Of course,' he said eventually. 'We will set off as soon as we can. About an hour, okay?'

Kate gripped the phone tight. 'That would be good, thanks.'

Kate looked at the faces of Milly and Roger as she told them about Jamie's accident, and the circumstances that led to a mother telling a father to leave the bedside of their gravely injured son when he'd finally come back to the hospital.

Milly was pale, her lemon two-piece washing out her make-up even further. She looked like she might vomit, and Kate hated herself for doing this to them. Neil should be here to tell him. Be man enough to stand by his decisions, his mistakes. The wind was a slow breeze, at times taking the heat of the sun that shone down on the centre gardens. They were sat watching Cooper and Jamie play hoops in their chairs. Cooper was pretty steady walking but still a bit wobbly at times. Kate knew that the chair was more for Jamie's benefit. Their laughter carried across the grass to the wooden bench they were perched on.

Roger looked across at the laughter, and his stricken face melted into a smile.

'That Cooper – he really is good with him isn't he? I don't think I ever heard Jamie laugh like that before now.'

Kate nodded. He'd barely spoken to her since that day. He was still there for Jamie, though. Didn't let his hurt show, but she knew he felt her pushing him away. *I just need to make this right, hang in there with me.* 'He's had it tough, but I think we're through the worst of it now. I'm sick of being the bad guy here, but I can't tell Jamie the truth. It's made this whole thing so much harder. He hates me for keeping his dad away. I asked him to leave that day, but he didn't have to fall off the face of the Earth. I was angry when I found out what happened. Our marriage was over, but what he did... it cost Jamie. He'll be upset when it all comes out. I just want to get in front of it.'

Roger pursed his lips. 'We need to go and find him, today. Make him talk to his son and explain just what's going on. This is not the son we raised. No wonder he's been avoiding us. Lying. I tried contacting him at work again, but they're very tight-lipped. No wonder now, they're obviously protecting him.'

Kate shook her head. 'Not him they're protecting so much. I think it's her that they're trying to look after.' *An affair between colleagues wasn't exactly something they would want on stamped onto the company masthead.*

Milly still hadn't spoken; she was sitting looking down at her clasped hands. Roger nudged her gently, putting his arm around her.

'Milly love, we need to sort this out.'

Milly jerked her head to her husband, looking dazed.

'Milly, we need to go and find Neil,' he tried again. 'We need to sort this out, for Jamie.'

His wife looked at Jamie, who was playing hoops with some of the other soldiers now, chuckling as he passed one by with the ball in his lap.

Cooper was at Kate's side before she'd even realised he had moved.

'Kate, I overheard, and I don't want to cause any trouble, but...' He looked apologetic. 'I have an address for Neil. I know where he's living, if you want it.'

Roger answered before Kate could compute what he was saying to her. Looking at Cooper, she had the feeling that he had already been to that address.

'Yes, Cooper, we would. We can set off after lunch, catch him after work.' He looked at Kate and she nodded. 'Do you want to come with us Kate?'

Kate looked at Cooper, and he pulled her hand

into his, bringing it to his lips to kiss. She didn't stop him. Her hand welcomed the touch, needed it.

'I think you should,' he said softly. 'You need to see him again. I think once you see him, you'll know what to do.'

Kate shook her head. 'It won't make a difference, Cooper; Neil and I are over. I just want this dealt with, so Jamie and I can move on.'

She saw Cooper's jaw flex. Roger steered a fragile looking Milly over to the court to see Jamie, and Cooper took a seat across from her, not letting her hand go.

'Won't make a difference to anything? Not even us?'

'Cooper,' she replied, looking at their entwined fingers. 'All of this is too much for you, it's not fair. It's just too messy, and you don't know everyth—'

'I already told you, I'm in. I know none of this is easy, but I am all in here. For you and Jamie. I don't care about the other stuff, we can sort it, together.'

Kate pulled her hand away from his. 'I can't put you through this any more. I need to be selfish and concentrate on Jamie, and I don't know how bad this is going to get. Neil won't be happy that I involved his parents.'

Cooper shook his head. 'Jamie is my priority too,

which is why we're on the same page. I just can't help feeling that you're still holding back on me. There must be some other reason for us not to be together. Do you not love me? Is that it?'

'Don't you get it? I can't do this!' she half yelled at him. He didn't flinch, just kept looking at her with those piercing green eyes. She leant in closer. 'They don't even know everything, because I just can't be the one to tell them. I can't do it!'

'Tell them what?' Cooper asked. 'Tell me, Kate. Please.'

Kate flinched, a sad smile on her face. 'So, you have been there. Did you meet them?'

'I saw a woman in the house, yes.' He thought of the bump. 'Was he on the phone to her when the accident happened? Is that why you sent him away? I get it, Kate. I'm here. I would never do that.'

Kate shook her head, and started to walk away. 'You went behind my back to get his address, which tells me that you wanted to check things out for yourself. Which means you had doubts. It makes this all the easier. I'm so sorry Cooper, but all I've ever done is cause you pain and trouble. I'll get Jamie to call you. Roger and Milly are going to take him in, they have a ground floor room they can convert to his room, just till I get a house sorted. Trevor is going to sort out the transfer and I will be staying on at the centre. I think we should just be friends, if we can.'

Cooper snorted. 'Friends?' Kate sighed, putting her head in her hands and his gut clenched. She was shutting down again. 'I don't want to be your friend! I want us to be together. Can't you see how fucked-up this is, after everything we have been through? Don't give up now.'

Cooper took her hands away from her face and wrapped them in his on the table.

'Look at me.' His voice broke a little, and she stubbornly kept her eyes down. 'Look at me!' he shouted.

She looked him straight in the eyes. 'Cooper, it's done. Please, respect my wishes. I'm doing it for your own good, trust me. Jamie is going to be a mess when this all comes out. You have your recovery, we still have to be here together, keeping it a secret. I just can't drag you through all that. I can't.'

Cooper shook his head, getting up. 'You do me a favour, Missy, you want to lie to yourself, you keep me out of it. I know the truth, so don't insult me.'

Kate watched him walk away, heading over to Jamie. Roger and Milly looked across at her but said nothing. They didn't say anything in the car either, all the way to the address Cooper had given them.

Pulling up at the house, Kate saw Roger check the

address written on the sheet. He turned off the engine and frowned at the sat nav.

'It seems we're here; he must be renting?'

Kate shrugged. 'I don't know, maybe.'

Milly was staring at something through the window of the house. She looked haunted; she had all morning since Kate had broken the news. Roger kept shooting her worried glances, and Kate once again silently cursed her feckless ex-husband for being such a coward. Not that she was any better. She had just stamped all over Cooper's heart, and her chance of being a family with a man she loved. The first and only man she had ever truly loved and cared for.

Roger nodded to himself and squeezed his wife's hand.

'Come on then, let's go and see our son.'

The knock at the door caused a dog to bark, and the three of them shifted from foot to foot as they heard shuffling coming from inside. The door opened, a woman's voice ringing out.

'Barney, sshh! I'm sorry, he's no guard dog, I can tell you. Might lick you to death, though.'

The woman was pretty, Kate could see from over Roger's shoulder. She recognised her from the company profile page, although they had never met.

Funny how someone you'd never even spoken to could have such a reach in your life.

She was looking at Roger and Milly expectantly, her face so open and friendly. She obviously had no idea who they were. Kate decided to test a theory. Stepping forward, out from behind Roger, she flashed a smile. The woman's smile vanished, her eyes darting from face to face.

'Hi,' Kate trilled. 'Is my ex-husband here?'

The woman paled. 'Er, yes he is... just, er... I'm sorry – I'll get him.'

'You do that.'

The woman turned to head back into the house, but was cut off by a figure. Neil was standing there, a look of shock plastered across his features.

Kate grinned at him, feeling her chest hammering with the simmering anger she felt inside. If he hadn't got his pregnant partner standing next to him, she felt sure she could have launched herself at him like a wildcat. All teeth and fur flying. She wanted to rip him apart.

'Hi. I came to talk about your firstborn. Remember him?'

Neil flapped his lips like a fish struggling for breath, and the woman swiftly disappeared into a room, closing the door behind her. Neil didn't seem to know what to do with his arms, he kept crossing and uncrossing them. Milly started to cry, and Roger put his arm around her.

'Neil?' he said to his son. 'I think you had better let us in, unless you want to do this on your doorstep.'

Neil looked at his dad and moved aside. 'Come in.'

The room was clean and tidy, decorated in light tones and with minimal clutter. It was actually quite homely, even Kate had to acknowledge it was a nice home. *Her* home, Kate could tell. Her husband had landed right on his feet. In one corner of the room, she could see a baby play gym boxed up in the corner. Milly was at the mantelpiece, a picture of the pair of them in her hands. Neil was standing at the doorway, as though he needed to be near the exit. Typical Neil. Roger sat in the chair, looking around the room in obvious disgust. Kate perched herself on the end of the sofa.

'Mum?' Neil ventured. Milly turned to look at him, thrusting the frame in his direction. Neil threw her a rueful smile, but the usually quiet woman exploded.

'Don't you smile at me, you disgusting man. You left your son fighting for his life while you ran to the side of your pregnant fancy piece?'

'Mum, it wasn't like that. What could I do? Jamie had people with him. I was in bad shape. When I got the call in the car telling me she was pregnant, I panicked. The doctors sent me home, so I came here. I didn't cheat, Mum, Kate and I were over. I made a mistake. I lost control of the car when she told me. I caused the accident. I came here to check on things, and when I went back and told Kate, she kicked me out! I had to make a choice.'

Kate snorted. 'Oh, you made that alright, but you seem to have made all the wrong choices since. I made you leave because I was angry, but I tried to get in touch with you. You packed up your shit before Jamie was even out of danger. I came home that night to an empty house! You should have been there. Not for me, for him!'

'I'm sorry. I can't tell you how sorry I am. I can't even look Jamie in the face. I thought he'd heard, in the car. I panicked, the car came out of nowhere, or I swerved.' He was rambling now, looking from face to face and finding no sympathy. 'I fucked up. I want to be there for him. I call him, but I can't face him. I can't tell him this, I can't. I put him in that chair. I was lonely, and you were in Iraq – I—'

'I don't want to hear it. I just came to tell you that I'm not covering for you any more. I have Jamie covered, but you need to step up and own...' She waved her hands around her. 'This. We were done a long time ago, Neil, and all I want from you is that.' She turned to his parents, who looked like they were about to pass out. 'Roger, Milly, I'm sorry it had to happen like this. I'll make my own way home.'

She was halfway down the drive when Neil came after her. He grabbed her arm, and she pushed him off.

'Get the hell off me!' she screamed, pushing him hard in the chest. Neil dropped back, holding his hands up in surrender.

'I'm sorry! I get it, I just wanted to know if Jamie is okay?'

His words earned him a slap around the face. She slapped him as hard as she could, and he took it. They both stood there, breathing hard. Kate's hand stung from the slap. It felt good. She wished she could do it again, but she had the feeling she wouldn't stop. No good for anyone.

'How dare you ask me that? I know I sent you away, but when I found out you were distracted on that call, and why? I lost it. I'd just stepped off a plane from a warzone! I was blindsided, angry. Upset. You should have done better. Been better, taken better care of him. You guilt-tripped me for weeks when I was working out there, and you were doing what? Shagging your colleague? Neil, you caused that crash, and then you left our son alone while you went to see your new family. Who does that?'

Neil gritted his teeth. 'I was there, Kate. For months before, years. Looking after him while you were off doing your own thing.'

'I was working! Doing important things like saving lives, I didn't abandon him like you did!' She sank into herself, a deep sigh erupting from within. 'I said what I needed to. I need to get back to the centre.'

'Can I see him?' he asked. 'I need to see him, I know I need to explain things. I'm so sorry, I will make this right, I promise.'

Kate wanted to tell him to go to hell, to see his face crumble when she informed him that he would never set eyes on their son again, but then she thought of Jamie and the words stuck in her throat.

'If you see him, you have to tell him everything. I mean it, you can't hide any more. I have protected you enough, but I do owe you that. It's not about us, it's about him.'

Neil nodded and Kate started to walk away.

'Kate, will you thank the man that came, in the chair? I assume that he was the one who told you where I was. I know I'm a coward, but I am glad to talk. Own up. I'm not this guy, Kate. You know that. I was just messed up, I acted out. I didn't think any of this would happen. It's been killing me, all this. I didn't know what to do.' He sagged before her. 'He was right. I need to do better. For this baby, and Jamie. For you. He was right.'

Kate didn't answer, she headed down the street as fast as she could walk. Not for the first time, she realised that Cooper really was all in. He'd known everything and had still wanted forever. She just wished that she could be the uncomplicated woman he deserved. Wished she hadn't hurt him by trying to save him from the mess he was already fully aware of. She should have known better. His event was so close now, he'd worked so hard. Going to him now, when all of this was going on? No. She would stay away, be his friend. Go with him to the ball, support him. For everything he had done, for her, for Jamie – she would push aside her feelings, and be by his side.

24

They walked into the ballroom side by side, but the gulf between them could have made the Grand Canyon look like a crack in the pavement. It felt wretched, and Kate was constantly battling the sting of tears. The last thing she wanted to do was break down and show him up in front of everyone. She wanted to be here for him, see him through this evening. Be his rock for once.

Since the day she had seen Neil, things had been better for Jamie. Neil had come to the centre with his parents, and told him the truth. Things had been rough, but Neil and Jamie were in contact with each other, and tentative steps had been taken. Baby steps, as she told Jamie. Sometimes, it took a while to get to where you needed to be. Jamie had hugged her tight. She had her boy back, finally. Cooper had been there for him, a sounding board for his confusion and anger. Things were better, Jamie was living with his grandparents till the house sale was complete, and she was getting back to normal at work. Whatever normal was before. The only thing missing now was Cooper, and Kate was broken without him. She wanted to talk to him, to explain how she felt, but she wouldn't put him in the crosshairs of the complications again.

They had skirted around each other in the centre. The only conversations they had were when Jamie was present for his physio, and Cooper kept himself to himself when she saw him around the centre. The only personal contact she'd had was a text asking her if she would still come with him tonight, as his date. So here they were. A night of champagne and silent yearning. Perfect.

The room was huge, all lit by strategic soft lighting. The ceiling was festooned in cream silky swathes of fabric, gathered together in the middle and splayed out to the corners of the room. It looked magnificent, and Kate was glad that she had made the extra effort with her outfit. She felt a chill despite the candles lighting up the tables, and she saw Cooper flinch as he caught her shiver. He turned his head to look at her bare arms.

'Cold?' he muttered. She nodded numbly. His lips were pinched tight, as though he was trying to hold every word of his to ransom against her. He started to shrug off his jacket, and she went to grab his arm.

'No, Cooper, you don't have to,' she said, and a tear fell out onto her cheek. She couldn't bear him like this, being nice, but coiled up. Detached. It was hard to be in his presence and not tell him she longed to be his. She just wanted him to be clear-headed, focused on his night. She was clearly doing an excellent job so far: Cooper looked stricken. He pulled her to the side of the room. Hightower shouted to him, but Cooper shook his head at him so he turned back to the bar with his date. Cooper pulled her to him so people wouldn't overhear. He looked upset, concerned, and Kate tried to brush away the tear without ruining the make-up job. He wiped her face with his fingers, gripping her chin gently to get her to look at him. She looked into his eyes and smiled in apology.

'I'm sorry, I didn't mean to—'

'Do you want to be with me, Kate? Tonight, I mean,' he clarified, sadness etching his features.

'Yes, of course I do,' she said softly, taking his hand in hers. He gripped it tight in return.

'Good, because I want you to be. Why are you crying?'

Damn it, just tell him. Just tell him now. Screw it. Worst case, you'll be home in a few hours and it will be over.

'Because I care, Cooper. I thought I could stand the distance between us, but it's awful. I hurt you, and I keep hurting you. I love you so much, I'm so proud of you, Thomas. I'm just so sad that I messed up.'

She didn't say another word because Cooper had pulled her into his arms and kissed her. He kissed her like he had been waiting his whole life to do it, and couldn't wait another minute. She sank into him, feeling the heat in the pit of her stomach. He turned her around in his arms, pushing her closer to the ball-room wall, tripping over his own feet to move her to him. They were still kissing each other, her hands in his hair when they heard a pronounced cough behind them, and a girlish giggle.

Kate turned around and felt Cooper chuckle as he tucked her into his side.

'Awesome timing as always, man,' he said to his buddy. Hightower was stood there, looking decidedly uncomfortable under his smile.

'Sorry, but I thought you were going to set the

sprinklers off.' He smiled ruefully. 'Smithy's wife is here. She wants to see you.'

Cooper visibly tensed and Kate gave him a squeeze. She was convinced he was going to fall over at one point, with his body seeming to sway, but he steadied himself. The shake in his hands was evident when he reached up to straighten his already perfect bow tie and tuxedo jacket.

'Did she bring the boys?' His voice came out like a plea. Hightower shook his head. 'No, mate, just his mother.' Cooper took no solace in those words. The woman standing with Hightower stepped forward hurriedly, awkwardly holding out a hand to Kate.

'Shall we go sit, let these two boys go mingle?' She had bright red nails, which matched her pillar box-red dress and kitten heels. It matched her flame-red hair, and the whole effect with the sparkle from the candle-light made her look like she was on fire. Kate looked to Cooper to check he was okay, but she saw he wasn't next to her any more. Not really. He was back with Smithy, on that bullet-ridden street far away. She took the woman's hand and walked away towards the ta-bles. She looked over her shoulder at Hightower, and saw he was talking in Cooper's ear. Probably talking the demons out of his head. Kate wondered for the millionth time about the cost of war. Did anyone truly win? Judging from the energy in this room, it was mankind's spirit that endured, sure, but not without ghosts.

The woman in red was pulling her along through the tables, seemingly knowing where she was heading. She glanced over her shoulder, flashing pearly-white teeth.

'You're sitting with us,' she stated, answering a question Kate hadn't found the breath to voice yet. She pointed to a table near the corner, and Kate could see Cooper's and her names on matching place cards. The sight of them made her feel all warm and fuzzy, and she had to stop herself from rubbing them together making kissy noises. The way he had kissed her had told her that he hadn't given up... but what would happen next?

The woman turned to her, holding two glasses of champagne that she had grabbed from a passing waiter's tray.

'Here, get that down you. He'll be okay, I promise. Brad does that sometimes too, he talks himself off the ledge half the time. He can help Coop. I'm Ruth, by the way, Brad's wife.'

Kate frowned, puzzled.

'Hightower,' Ruth said, pulling a face as if to say this happened a lot. 'Army wife, sorry – I should know by now that they never use their actual names. Or is that just men in general?' She shrugged in answer to her own question, gesturing for Kate to sit. 'So, how long have you and Coop been seeing each other now? Brad's always tight-lipped about the ladies his mates date. I swear, I don't know what they talk about.'

She flicked her long red hair back from her face, and Kate noticed she had a long surgery scar down one side of her neck. Ruth saw her looking and flicked a nail down the silvery line.

'Liking my battle scar? I bet you could have done a better job, but hey, it was done in the field – better than bleeding out. I have to keep my hair long, but it doesn't bother me.'

Kate nodded, looking away. 'Sorry, I was just surprised. Did you serve?'

'Field medic. We got attacked, one guy tried to take our medicine supply. I tried to stop him, to save it for the patients that needed it. He slashed me, left me for dead. Bastard.'

She drained her glass, and Kate recognised the dulling of her eyes. How many battlefield spectres were there present in this room? She finished her glass off too, and Ruth grinned at her.

'Sorry, oversharer. Another?' She said, and Kate

nodded, feeling the first buzz of alcohol warm her churning stomach. *I like this woman.*

Ruth stood to get the attention of a passing waiter, and Kate saw that she had clocked something across the room. Ruth sat back down, pulling her chair a little closer to Kate and taking her hands in hers.

'Don't look, but Cooper is talking to Smithy's wife. I know they're both nervous about it, but honestly, she just wants to thank him.'

Kate cringed. 'Thanking him will do him more harm than good. He blames himself.'

Ruth patted her hand, and the two women looked at each other. They understood each other, and Kate was glad to have met her.

'You got any kids?' Kate asked her, nodding towards Hightower.

Ruth snorted, winking at the waiter as she emptied the tray he lowered to her. 'Thanks, doll,' she said cheekily. Kate thought she might smack him on the bottom as he walked off, the way she looked at him, but she just waggled her eyebrows at Kate. Her shocked expression sent Ruth into fits of giggles.

'Come on, the man is lush! He could make a pretty penny if he lost the rest of the penguin suit and just stuck to the apron.' Kate's jaw dropped.

'Hey,' Ruth tittered. 'I love Brad, he is my one and

only, but life is short. I can appreciate the cut of a nice-looking man once in a while. They sure as hell do it to us. Being in your profession, as a woman, you should get that, surely.'

Kate nodded, seeing the sense of what she was saying. 'True.'

'Truth is, I haven't talked about kids with Brad yet. I want them, sure, now I'm based here. I took a desk job after the last tour. Brad is still going back out there though, and I know he worries about leaving a child without a father.'

She cast her eyes over to the men, who were deep in conversation with a small blonde woman. She looked like she could be blown over by a good gust of wind. Kate could see her eyes as she spoke to Cooper. She recognised the haunted expression on her face. She had seen it many times. More often than not, though, it was on the dying. It was what a person looked like when hope was gone. Having nearly lost her son, and watching him struggle without his father, she could see Brad's point.

'What do *you* want?' Kate turned back to Ruth, taking the flute that was thrust at her and taking another sip. She could feel the bubbles going down her throat, rolling over her stomach knots and massaging out the kinks.

'I am thirty-six, hun, the time for turkey basting and egg freezing is almost upon us. I want to get cracking, but I don't want to force him into something he can't commit to in his heart. He wants kids, they all do, but it's the job. It changes you, it hardens you somehow. The last thing I want is for my husband to be distracted when he's fighting for his life, miles from home. So, I don't push. He's considering leaving himself, but it needs to be his decision. When I got hurt, we'd been engaged for a month. I came home, and we got married then and there. He didn't even really ask; it was just arranged. Cooper pretty much did everything but be a flower girl to help, too. The man is a prickly pear, but he's a diamond too.'

Kate looked across at him, but they were all gone. She hoped it was going well, wherever they had gone to. The ballroom was building to a high volume of voices, and people were milling around, doing interviews for the press, posing for photos, chatting and laughing as the warmth of the room and the alcohol took hold.

'You have a son, right? Cooper says he's in the facility?'

Ruth's voice snapped her back to their conversation. 'Yes, Jamie. He is in the facility, yes, in the day, but we're hoping to move on soon. I need to find some-where nearby that can accommodate us.'

Ruth nodded. 'Cooper said you were looking. Give me a shout if you get stuck, my sister is an estate agent. The woman is ferocious too. How is he doing?'

Kate sighed. 'He's okay. It was rough for a long time, but Cooper helped. He was amazing.'

'Well, I know he loves him to bits.' Ruth smiled. 'I was kind of hoping it might rub off on Brad. Sorry,' Ruth held up her hands. 'Two glasses of this stuff and I turn into Oprah.'

'No, no it's fine,' Kate smiled. 'It's nice that he talks to someone. Him and Brad are close, it's good.'

Kate threw the contents of her glass down her throat, waving her finger teasingly at the waiter, who blushed and started to walk over.

'Sometimes, I can't tell whether I just married Brad, or adopted them both. Let's get pissed, eh? The awards are bound to be sooo dull.'

Kate was about to answer when she felt hands touch her bare shoulders. She looked up and Cooper was there. He dropped a tender kiss on her lips, licking his own after.

'Hmm, champagne,' he murmured, smiling at her. He looked pale, and she could see the pain in his eyes, but she didn't show any reaction. She reached up and ran her palm along his cheek. He turned and kissed it. Whatever else happened, they had this. She let the touch of her warm him, soothe him in their own special way.

'Did I hear talk of getting drunk?' Hightower said, flopping into the chair next to Ruth, almost spilling his pint into her lap. She swatted at him, and he pretended to snap at her with his teeth. She rolled her eyes, putting her hand on his knee. Cooper sat down next to her, motioning to the long-suffering waiter. Kate flashed him an apologetic smile. The poor guy looked relieved that they had men sitting with them.

Ruth leaned forward, laughing. 'He thinks we're cougars,' she said. Brad cracked out laughing. Cooper looked annoyed, and Kate laughed, despite herself.

'Keep your pants on, Coop, the woman is not for turning,' Ruth said, and Cooper stuck his tongue out.

'Good,' he said, putting his arm around her. 'Because I think she's already spoken for.' He leaned in, giving her a kiss on her cheek, and whispered in her ear. 'What's going on? Is this you seeing sense?' He looked at her and she saw the hopeful optimism in his green eyes. 'Are you going to try?'

'I want to but I don't want to drag you into some part-time thing. I have work, and Jamie.'

His eyes narrowed. 'So all this has been about protecting me, because you think you have baggage?' He spoke low, but their friends were engrossed in conversation anyway, giving them space.

'Yes,' Kate said. 'I asked you to live your life, to fight, and you did. I don't want to get in the way of that.'

Cooper nodded, dropping a kiss onto her lips. 'Okay. Good to know.'

* * *

The night went a little smoother from there. Cooper seemed to relax a little, and Kate was aware of his presence near her at all times. He always made an excuse to touch her in some way, his hand on hers, or the brush of his arm against the top of her own. She felt as though he wanted to say something to her, but couldn't find the words. She could relate. They skirted around each other with their bodies instead, doing a silent dance that made Kate's every nerve ending tingle. Ruth and Brad were a great couple, and if they picked up on anything amiss between their dinner companions, they didn't show it. They laughed and joked through dinner, the other people at their table all being swept along with the conversation. Ruth was a hoot, and Brad's one-liners and her witty retorts made the whole table erupt with laughter.

The meal was beautiful and the wine was flowing. Kate didn't want to lose her head, but after drinking with Ruth earlier, she was feeling a tad on the tipsy side. Looking at Cooper, she tried to see if he was on her wavelength but she just couldn't tell. He looked like the same old Cooper, steady as a rock.

Soon the meal was over, and the speeches part of the evening was underway. The whole room fell silent, but Kate noticed a good few of the men in uniform gravitated to the bar. *Dutch courage.* Cooper looked across at them, and then at Brad. Brad said nothing but kissed Ruth on the cheek and stood up from the table. Walking over to the bar, the men saw him coming and parted for him. Kate glanced over at Cooper, and he was looking right at her.

'Our bit's up next. The guys at the bar are my unit. I'll introduce you later.' He clenched his jaw and Kate reached for his hand. He grabbed at it, gripping it tight. 'Thanks for being here.'

Kate reached up and touched his face with her palm. He turned his face to kiss it, and she felt the graze of stubble against her skin. 'I wouldn't be anywhere else.'

He smiled at her, and she realised the look he was

giving her was something she had seen many times from him before. Today though, she knew what it meant. The man was in love. With her. Had been for a while. He was still right there with her, and she knew that after tonight, she wouldn't let him go. She'd love him for the rest of her life, come what may.

'Next on the agenda this evening,' the announcer's voice cut through the room. 'We honour a man who has a decorated service record and has done no less than three tours in overseas conflict, and countless other missions, leading his own crack unit. In the last tour of Iraq, his unit came under heavy fire. The officer's quick actions saved the unit, civilians, and lessened the loss of life. We honour him tonight, and also the loss of one of his officers, Sergeant Smith. Adam Smith gave his life for the safety and protection of our country, and we are humbled to share the honouring of these men with their families. Tonight, we honour the late Adam Smith, and Captain Thomas Cooper. Thomas, could you come up here please?'

Kate felt his hand tighten around hers, and then it was gone.

The announcer seemed to be studying his notes intently, and he blustered a little.

'I don't know... er... do we need to... does someone want to give Mr Cooper some assistance to the stage?'

In the darkness of the room, Kate could see the guests looking nervously around them, and she couldn't see Cooper. Her heart was in her mouth. She looked at Ruth, but she was looking at the stage. Kate scanned the bar frantically, her blonde hair coming loose a little from her pin up. She looked at the faces but they were all facing a spot halfway between her and the stage. She looked to where they were pointing and there he was. He was walking towards the stage, shoulders back straight. The murmur of voices around the room buzzed louder, till the announcer waved his hands to quieten them down. Of course, the crowd ignored him, so he kept flapping his hands ineffectually.

The audience were all transfixed, clapping and following the man whose presence swelled the room itself, but Kate didn't see any of that. All she saw was Cooper. Her Cooper. His face looked relaxed, a smile playing on his lips as he walked slowly but confidently across the room towards the stage. To the onlookers, he was a symbol of hope, out there proving to people that people survived, people endured. The protective surge of love she felt in her heart felt like it was going to knock her off her feet. She was glad to be sat on a chair, gripping the back rest for dear life. He neared the stage and Kate wanted to scoop him up from the world and put him in her pocket. He was hers and she had never loved anything or anyone more in her life, aside from Jamie. She could see his jaw flexing and she wondered how nervous and terrified he actually was, walking up to that stage in front of his family. His real family, the one he had never had as a child. She wondered if he was glad to be alive, even in that moment. He had lost so much, but did he truly see now what he had gained?

He made the stairs easily, the sounds of the applause from the crowd ringing in his ears.

He shook the announcer's hand, moving to the front of the podium. Two awards stood next to the microphone, each depicting a soldier in full kit, standing to attention. Cooper stood looking at them for a moment, before reaching out to pick one up.

He held it out in his fist, nodding towards Smithy's family.

'Having a piece of metal and plastic in your house as a reward for someone giving his life always seemed a little crass to me.' The audience fell silent, and Kate held her breath. Glancing across at Hightower, she saw his lips twitch. She knew what he was thinking. Typical Cooper. She looked back to him, and they locked eyes. Kate felt the familiar slam in his chest as she looked at him, and she mouthed, 'I love you', before she could even think about it. He smiled broadly at her, causing a few people to turn their heads towards her. She kept her eyes on him, ignoring the inquisitive looks she could feel on her face. He looked again at Smithy's wife and took a breath.

'It might sound harsh, what I just said, when I'm the one standing here, and Smithy isn't. The truth is, losing him was unbearable to me, for a long time, as it was for many others sitting here. Losing a brother is something that I dreaded the most. It's why we're all there, fighting for our families, and to keep each other safe. Smithy was a great soldier, and I couldn't save him, and that's something that I can't forgive myself for.' His voice broke a little, and Kate's eyes welled up. She dug her nails into her palms as hard as she could. She would not cry, she would be strong, a solid support system for him. Just like he had been for her and Jamie all these months.

'Awards never meant much to me before that day, and today I stand here saying thank you – for me, and for Smithy. I know he would have got a kick out of this, and I know his family are proud. I'm honoured to have known him, and the rest of my team.' He put down the award and picked up its matching partner, running his finger along the gold plaque at the base.

'And with my award, I've decided to honour

someone else. The truth is, after the explosion, I didn't want to live.' The sound of the audience cut off, as if someone had muted the volume. Kate could hear nothing but the beating of her head over heels heart. 'In fact, I was adamant that I was done. Hightower and a few others here know what I'm like when I get my head on.' A burble of laughter rippled across the room, and Cooper fake scowled at them, causing more deep chortles.

'My award is dedicated to a stubborn, fiery woman who came into my world on the worst day of my life and forced me to fight. She forced me to fight my body, my mind, and even on occasion, her. The woman has a tongue like a rattlesnake and is as stubborn as an ox, but she was right.' The audience lapped it up, laughter and soppy grins all around the room. 'Life for me was the army, I thought it would only ever *be* the army. She showed me that I had other things to live for. I will never leave the field of battle. Everyone here left a piece there, one way or another, and I can live with that. Because Doctor Kate Harper taught me how.'

He looked down at the award in his hands, and then back at her. 'I love you for that Kate, and many other reasons. So thank you, from the bottom of my heart.'

Hightower whooped loudly as the audience sprang

to life. Ruth nudged Kate, clapping. 'Check you out, Dr Harper!'

Cooper leaned into the microphone. 'Kate, I am here, and I'm all in. Marry me.'

The audience gasped and the noise abruptly cut off. Everyone was looking agog from Cooper to Kate, and she felt a tear drop onto her cheek.

Captain Thomas Cooper, the most stubborn, masculine man she had ever met was standing in front of everyone he loved, pouring his heart out and declaring his love. She knew then and there what her answer was, and what it always would be.

'Yes,' she said, running to the stage as the audience erupted. He met her at the stairs, and when they crushed their bodies together, he whispered in her ear. 'You're stuck with me now, Missy.'

EPILOGUE
TWO YEARS LATER

'Jamie, dude – get a move on, your transport is on the way!' Kate was walking through the house, picking up a discarded half-chewed sock that Jamie's dog had eviscerated. She gave the mischievous labrador a stern look as he looked suitably guilty from his basket in her son's room.

'Buddy, this is not cool. Socks are not toys!'

Jamie laughed from his chair as he grabbed his backpack and threw his pencil case into a zip pocket. 'He ate three yesterday too. He loves the smell of your feet!'

Kate kissed her son, rolling her eyes. Jamie was back in school and living in their adapted bungalow made life so much easier. He had his struggles, but he was happy. He even saw his dad once a month, although things were a little strained. Like Cooper said, 'it's a work in progress.'

'Taxi's here,' Cooper said, coming into the hallway. 'I finish work at the centre early today, and your mum has a late surgery, so shall I pick you up, we can go shoot some hoops?' He pretended to make a basket with his hands.

'That's it, old man, get some practice in, I am so not going easy on you!' Jamie clipped his pack onto his chair, fist-bumping Cooper on his way out of the door.

'Bye, Mum, Dad, love you!' The door shut behind him, and Kate and Cooper looked at each other in shock.

'Did you hear that?' Cooper said. 'He called me Dad!'

Kate wrapped her arms around her husband, pulling him as close to her as she could manage.

'I know,' she said, peppering his face with kisses. 'Might as well get used to it.'

He kissed her back, his stubble rubbing her cheek as he knelt down. Putting both hands on her baby bump, he kissed her tummy.

'I can manage that,' he said, looking up at her with a grin that made her heart sing and her stomach flip. 'Best job I ever had.'

ACKNOWLEDGEMENTS

Huge thanks to Emily Ruston and the whole amazing team at Boldwood for bringing another title out into the world and giving it all the love and expertise that they so effortlessly bestow to each story. Big thanks to my physiotherapist, Matt, from The Sandal Clinic in Wakefield, who not only fixed my tricky back some years ago, but answered my many questions and gave me pointers on sources for the medical parts of this book. Thanks also to the British Army and Help for Heroes for their information, and their service.

A huge helping of gratitude as always to my lovely family of authors, readers and bloggers, who spur me on and inspire me every day. There are too many of you to list, but a big mwah to you all. I love to hear from readers, and I hear such lovely comments. Thank you.

Lastly, as always a massive thank you to my family, especially my husband, Peter, and our sons Jayden and

Nathan. Thank you for putting up with the piles of clean washing everywhere and takeaway food while I tap away on my laptop for so many hours. I love you all.

ABOUT THE AUTHOR

Rachel Dove lives in leafy West Yorkshire with her family, and rescue animals Tilly the cat and Darcy the dog (named after Mr Darcy, of course!). A former teacher specialising in Autism, ADHD and SpLDs, she is passionate about changing the system and raising awareness/acceptance. She loves a good rom-com, and the beach!

Sign up to Rachel Dove's mailing list here for news, competitions and updates on future books.

Visit Rachel's website: www.racheldovebooks.co.uk

Follow Rachel on social media:

X x.com/writerdove

instagram.com/writerdove

facebook.com/racheldoveauthor

tiktok.com/@writerdove

ALSO BY RACHEL DOVE

Ten Dates

Summer Hates Christmas

Mr Right Next Door

The Long Walk Back

LOVE NOTES

LOVE IN EVERY CHAPTER

WHERE ALL YOUR ROMANCE
DREAMS COME TRUE!

THE HOME OF BESTSELLING
ROMANCE AND WOMEN'S
FICTION

 WARNING:
MAY CONTAIN SPICE

SIGN UP TO OUR
NEWSLETTER

https://bit.ly/Lovenotesnews

Boldwood

Boldwood Books is an award-winning fiction publishing company seeking out the best stories from around the world.

Find out more at www.boldwoodbooks.com

Join our reader community for brilliant books, competitions and offers!

Follow us
@BoldwoodBooks
@TheBoldBookClub

Sign up to our weekly deals newsletter

https://bit.ly/BoldwoodBNewsletter

www.ingramcontent.com/pod-product-compliance
Lightning Source LLC
Chambersburg PA
CBHW010702100726
47900CB00010B/2761